*This story is dedicated to all those who have ever dealt with a bully. Keep your chin up, believe in yourself, and persevere!*

# BEFORE BECOMING A MAN

## A NOVEL

# JESS QUINN

*Enjoy!*

ISBN: 978-0-9854327-4-4
Ebook ISBN: 978-0-9854327-5-1

*Book design by Justin Fulton*
*Author photograph by Smith Photography*

AfterWords Books website: www.awbooks.co
Printed in the United States of America

AfterWords
BOOKS

*A special thank you to Mr. John Zahoran, whose knowledge of the English language and American literature intimidated me in Eighth Grade and astounds me still today, and for believing that "We might have something here."*

*To my wife Heather; children Devon, Aidan and Brady, for your love and patience.*

*Finally, to all the students at Clarion Area Elementary for your enthusiasm and support and for always inspiring me to keep writing.*

# 1

"Let's go!"

Ryan heard a loud and familiar voice coming from downstairs.

"Come on Ryan, get a move on!" the voice demanded.

Ryan's eyes popped open as he jumped out of bed and raced down the hallway. Reaching the stairwell, he bounded downward, his feet hitting every other step until reaching the bottom.

Ryan fell asleep early the night before and didn't hear his father come home. His dad had been out of town on business. Ryan didn't have a chance to say goodbye before his father left for the station and boarded the train headed to Washington D.C. He was very excited as he hit the kitchen floor and threw himself into his father's arms.

His dad was a large man. Everywhere they went, people knew him. He was well respected throughout the neighborhood. His father was like Superman, seemingly capable of doing anything and doing it well. He was tall and broad across his back with chiseled shoulders hard as a rock. As large and broad as he was across the shoulders, he had the slimmest of waists. His legs were long, muscular, and athletic. Jet-black hair, thick and wavy, covered his head. He was rugged yet refined.

Ryan, on the other hand, was just the opposite. He was short and could stand to gain a few pounds. He always referred to himself as being vertically challenged. Ryan was so small in stature that he was constantly challenged by every kid in the neighborhood. Even the ones younger than Ryan took turns picking on him. Ryan's main strength was his ability to read - and read he could.

Being squeezed by his father was the best and yet most painful experience. The scene quickly turned sour for Ryan, however, as his father insisted they go to the backyard to play catch. He enjoyed spending time with his dad, but he didn't enjoy the activity. It was always something physical; catch with a baseball and glove or a football. Ryan spent much of the time running after the balls he dropped or completely missed altogether. His father was an avid outdoorsman. Hunting, fishing, and hiking were activities that were high on his list of things to do when time permitted.

His dad was fast! Once Ryan witnessed him chase down and catch a small rabbit that had been trapped inside their fenced in back yard. The rabbit zigged, his father zagged. Within a few minutes, he had it cradled in his enormous hands. Shelly, Ryan's sister had a cat that surely would have hunted the rabbit down if his father didn't save it first.

Trips to the shooting range never ended well for Ryan. He couldn't hold the gun steady enough to hit the target. This past fall was the worst. Sandbags were set up on the shooting bench so Ryan didn't have to hold the rifle steady. He was told to grip the handle and the forearm of the gun tightly. Then his father instructed him to close his left eye and stare into the rifle's scope.

"I can't see anything," Ryan told his father.

"Move your eye closer so that you can see the field of vision," his father insisted. "Can you see the target, yet?"

"Yes," Ryan replied.

"When you have lined up the crosshairs of the scope on the bullseye, gently squeeze the trigger."

Gently, Ryan squeezed. BOOM! The rifle roared and Ryan fell backward holding his eye, his ears ringing. The recoil of the rifle shot back with such force that the weapon jumped out of Ryan's grip and the scope hit his eyebrow, cutting him slightly. A small butterfly bandage was all that was needed to close the wound.

Still his eye was swollen and bruised black and blue for a week. Fishing was no different. Ryan always ended up with a hook imbedded in his finger and his line in knots!

None of these activities appealed to Ryan. Even hiking didn't end well. He once tripped over roots on the trail and sprained his ankle.

Summoning up courage as he walked with his father to their backyard, Ryan asked a difficult question, one that had been on his mind for as long as he could remember.

"Dad," Ryan asked, head down, voice soft. "Why do we always do something I'm not good at?" He paused. "You know I can't catch and I can barely throw the ball far enough to get it back to you." He closed his eyes

Ryan's dad stared at the baseball for a short time, tossed it softly in the air, and then walked toward Ryan. He put his arm around his son and said, "I wasn't always as strong and confident as I am today." The two walked to the porch and sat together on the bottom step. He continued. "Soon Ryan, you will be on the verge of becoming a man."

Ryan laughed a little. His father finished. "You will need to step into a new role."

"What?" Ryan said as his face wrinkled. "Dad, I am 12 years old! I have a long way to go before I become a man."

The sweet aroma of cinnamon rolls coming from the kitchen piqued their interest. His mother called and Ryan quickly turned and went inside. His father, watching him go up the steps, said under his breath, "It will be sooner than you think, son." He walked slowly up the steps to join his son for a roll and glass of milk.

"Did you tell him, Robert?" Diane, Ryan's mother whispered to his dad.

"No, not yet," he said. "The time is not right. It may frighten him. Ryan is not ready to hear that sort of news."

"When?" she pressed.

"We will know when. That time is not now." His voice was stern and Ryan's mother knew that was the end of the conversation.

Ryan Donaldson was just like any other boy. He liked going on the computer, researching topics of interest and playing online games with people all over the world. He even liked playing with his plastic army men and spending time with his father when he was home.

Ryan's family lived in a small apartment in a western suburb of Philadelphia. His father traveled as a sales representative and had to spend much of his time out of town to support his family. Ryan's mother worked part-time at the local library, re-shelving books and keeping the periodicals updated.

Sitting at the table, enjoying a tall glass of ice cold milk and a steaming hot cinnamon roll dripping with melted icing, Ryan sat back in his chair and sighed, wishing he could tell his father about the troubles he was having at school.

"Everything going well at school, Ryan?" his father asked. But before he could answer, he scuffed Ryan's hair and said, "Good, glad to hear it," then disappeared into the living room, not giving Ryan a chance to answer.

The problems at school and the fact that he wasn't sleeping well again were becoming almost too much for Ryan to bear. He stared out the window remembering what it was like only a few short years ago. It was happening all over again.

When Ryan was 6 years old, he could be found awake, huddling in the corner of his bed in the middle of the night, crying for his mother. Ryan could remember everything about the nightmare that would awaken him so vividly. Almost a nightly occurrence, this dream would jolt him out of a deep sleep and startle him so that only the warmth of his mother's embrace would calm him. With Ryan's dad out of town on business much of the time, and Ryan being so young, his mother had no choice but to seek the advice of a counselor to help him make sense of this terrifying nightmare.

Ryan explained to his counselor in great detail the horrifying bear that stood before him in his nightmare, ready to strike him down. He clearly described the echoing roar of the great grizzly, the saliva dripping from its mouth, it's incredibly long teeth and claws. He could remember everything about the bear, down to the tear in its ear.

After many sessions, the therapist determined that the nightmare stemmed from the trouble Ryan had from a bully at daycare. He was picked on relentlessly by an 11-year-old boy and couldn't find the strength mentally or physically to defend himself.

Every afternoon, the school-aged children would ride the bus to their daycare, Counting Kids. Ryan was always dropped off close to noon as his kindergarten day covered the morning from 8 to 11:30 a.m. The older kids would arrive at 4 p.m. upon the conclusion of their day. On warm and sunny afternoons, the kids would be permitted to hit the playground. Every school-aged child stormed the fenced in area, squealing with excitement. The swings were taken first, then the monkey bars, and finally the jungle gym. All would be crawling with children.

The workers at the daycare were college students seeking degrees in education. They would congregate around the bench that was near the rear entrance of the building and wouldn't pay much attention to the kids as they played. This was where the trouble began. Brayden Johnson was a fifth grader who was very sly and able to manipulate situations at will. Most counselors thought he was a topnotch kid. When an employee was watching, Brayden would always gently push a younger child on the swing or give up his turn on the monkey bars. But when he was sure no one was paying attention, Brayden went right back to the dirty tricks, holding onto the swing and thus catapulting his victim through the air or gliding past smaller children on the monkey bars, bumping them to the ground without a second glance. When the younger boys and girls complained, they were told not to make up stories or that it wasn't polite to "tattle" on good students.

To say that Brayden did not like Ryan was a huge understatement. Ryan was the only kindergartener that Brayden never helped, no matter who was watching. Brayden was never openly aggressive, but all his friends knew he just had no time for a kid like Ryan. Every time Ryan would walk by, Brayden would scoff and purposely step into his way, causing him to fall to the ground, or Ryan would have to scramble and scurry out of the way to avoid a collision.

Things really took a turn for the worse when Ryan was playing with a small wind-up airplane he'd received from his father. Ryan was very proud of the gift. He would twist a rubber band around the propeller and then throw the plane high in the air. His plane would travel up to 25 feet on a single throw before gliding softly to the ground.

Brayden was sitting atop the jungle gym and noticed the small wooden aircraft gliding across the playground. With squinted eyes he slithered through the bars and casually made his way toward the grounded plane. Brayden got to the plane just as Ryan had bent down to pick it up.

CRUNCH!

Brayden stepped directly on the wing, snapping it in two. Immediately, Ryan's eyes filled with tears. Brayden's lip curled around his teeth as he grinned at Ryan. "Oops," he said.

Brayden quickly grabbed the plane from Ryan's hand and sprinted toward the doorway. "Miss Heller," Brayden called out. "I was playing and didn't watch where I was going. I stepped on this plane and it broke." Then he paused. "I'm sorry. I really didn't see it."

Ryan arrived at the doorway, eyes red and swollen, tears still dripping off his cheeks. "Miss Heller, that's my plane. Brayden stepped on it on purpose. I saw him."

Miss Heller looked at both boys standing before her. "Ryan, I know Brayden would do no such thing. You shouldn't be flying this here anyway!" she scolded. "You could put someone's eye out!"

Ryan was speechless. He began to cry harder.

"Go to the timeout chair and think about why you are there!" Miss Heller demanded.

Ryan was crushed. Not only did he get punished for someone else breaking his possession, but the plane itself was in pieces. He began to hate walking through the doors of Counting Kids.

The counselor gave Ryan a few tips to try to deal with this difficult situation. Her advice actually made things worse, as he came home one day with a swollen cheek and large bruises on his arms. That night Ryan had the dream again, woke and cried for his mother.

She later went so far as to speak to the manager of Counting Kids, but that again only made things worse. Afterwards, the supervisors blamed any spill or mess on Ryan. He was sent to the timeout chair for things he didn't do. When he protested, he was given even more time in the chair. He was made to feel like an outcast and the other children wanted nothing to do with him. Ryan felt completely alone.

Every night Ryan fought with his mother when it was time for bed. He did not want to sleep alone. He could only fall asleep if he went to bed clinging to his mother's side. She would wait for him to close his eyes and fall asleep. Then Mrs. Donaldson would carry him down the hallway to his bedroom. She wandered if this would ever end.

Finally, on a day when Ryan had enough, with his heart pounding and nostrils flared, he confronted the bully. One beautiful afternoon, the sun shining, not a cloud in the sky, the kids were released to the playground to let off some steam. Brayden overheard Miss Heller tell one of the other workers that she had to use the restroom and would be right out. Brayden grinned. Ryan darted behind the small climbing wall. The vagrant went straight for Ryan.

He pushed Ryan and asked, "Where's your plane? Oh, that's right, it's been permanently grounded!" Brayden laughed and laughed. Brayden's friends, who usually had his back, began to tell him to leave the kid alone. "C'mon man, let's go," they said.

Ryan became angry, madder than he had ever been in his life. With Brayden's head turned to acknowledge their comments, Ryan struck. He closed his eyes and with all his might kicked at the bully, dropping him to his knees. Brayden was caught off guard, but immediately regained his composure and slugged Ryan to the ground. Ryan did the only thing he could—he curled into a ball and remained motionless on the layers of mulch on the playground floor.

Something changed that day, however. Ryan didn't feel the expected thuds to his back or legs. He thought that maybe the supervisor had returned from the restroom, saving him from the beating. He was wrong. Brayden's comrades had turned on him. "Do you feel like a BIG MAN picking on a kindergartener?" Frustrated, Brayden walked away and left Ryan alone. From that moment on, Ryan was left to himself, not only at daycare, but also inside his own mind at night as he slept.

Mrs. Donaldson couldn't believe what she saw when

she opened his door one morning. Ryan was lying on his back, sleeping peacefully. She asked herself, "Could this be the end of the sleepless nights?" And it was, at least for the next few years. No nightmares, no crying, nothing to wake Ryan but the soft touch of his mother's hand.

From that moment on, Ryan enjoyed his time at daycare, often playing with small building blocks, and wasn't afraid to go to sleep in his own bed at night. Things were good and time passed quickly.

# 2

"I'm heading down to the deli on the corner. You wanna walk with me?" The voice of Ryan's father snapped him back to reality. The flashback was so strong that Ryan jerked both arms in the air, spilling what was left of his glass of milk on the kitchen table. Quickly he grabbed a paper towel and cleaned the mess.

"Sure," was his only reply.

Father and son strolled down the sidewalk on that April morning. The cherry trees that lined their street were in full blossom. The sweet smell, coupled with that of the freshly-cut grass, always made Ryan smile. Spring had arrived and summer was not far behind. He tried several times to tell his father about his recent troubles at school but was never given the opportunity. Even though he and his father had a very close relationship, Ryan couldn't find an opening to begin such a conversation. His father did most of the talking, telling him stories about when he was Ryan's age. He told stories of racing every kid on his street. He never lost! Not one race. He arm wrestled anyone who would take him on...and won every match. One time his father even dove for a thrown football and caught it.

Ryan asked, "What's the big deal with diving to catch a ball?"

"I dove on the street and caught it, Ryan. Scraped my elbows and knees terribly! But I caught it and scored a touchdown!" replied his father. "But it wasn't always like that for me. There was a time that none of the kids wanted anything to do with me."

"Why did things change for you?" Ryan asked.

"That is a conversation for another day," his father answered.

Ryan put his head down and stared at his feet as they strolled on. He didn't want his father to be ashamed of him. How could he tell his dad that he wasn't like him. In fact, Ryan's life was just the opposite. He got beat in every race, even by the girls. He never would think of entering an arm wrestling match. That looked like it would hurt! If he did go out to play, he was always the last to be picked. Nobody on the street wanted him to be on their team. If he did get picked, they didn't even talk to him during the game, as if he wasn't there.

The two walked into Conner's Deli and ordered some fresh sliced ham and steaming Kaiser rolls. Old man Conner came from behind the counter and personally handed Robert his order. "I threw in some extra rolls," he winked at Robert. "You shouldn't have," Robert said as he shook old man Conner's hand. Ryan's father insisted he pay for the extra rolls, but Mr. Conner wouldn't take it as he walked with them to the store entrance patting Robert's back as they left the store. It was perfectly clear to Ryan that old man Conner liked his father. The two chatted as they made their way back to their block. As they walked into the kitchen, Mrs. Donaldson took the fresh rolls and quickly made Ryan a sandwich. He retreated to his room to have his snack and opened his journal.

Ryan sat in his room and wrote. "My dad wants me to go and play with the other kids from the next street down. They are all bigger than me. They are stronger and faster than I am. Every game, I am the last one picked. Why does he make me do these things? Does my father know me at all?" He put his pencil on the desk and stared out the window. Ryan thought of his father and wondered how the two of them could be so different.

Everyone looked up to his dad. He once heard an older man talking to another describing his father. "He's built like a Greek God," the man said. Ryan had no clue what that meant, so he did a little research of his own. He saw pictures drawn of Greek soldiers whose bodies were chiseled to perfection, as if carved out of granite. Not an ounce of body fat present. These men held huge shields in one hand and a sharp sword in the other. Ryan read that each of these soldiers put his life on the line for the man who fought next to him. They fought as one. He thought of his father holding a shield and sword. Ryan wasn't sure if his father was built like a god, but he definitely could see his father as one of those soldiers.

# 3

Thinking about his situation in life made Ryan feel like he wasn't holding up his end of the bargain. He thought that his father would or should expect more from him. He just wasn't comfortable speaking out or standing up to the kids on his street. So he stayed quiet and kept to himself as much as possible. Everything had been moving smoothly for Ryan. The years came and went. He had no reason to think of the nightmare he had as a small child.

After a scuffle with a new boy at school, Ryan was again awakened by the terrible dream! Now 12, he faced the horrible nightmare once more. He couldn't believe that he could remember the dream with such detail.

Ryan, awake in his bed and staring at the ceiling, was startled as his alarm rang loudly in his ear. His clothes were soaked with sweat. He swung his feet over the edge of his bed and dropped them on the cold oak floor in his room.

6:30 a.m. was the worst time of the day. Ryan would

wake to begin another day of ridicule and humiliation. Finishing a very close second was 9:30 p.m., for that was the time his mother sent him to bed. Going to bed meant that morning would come all too quickly, not to mention Ryan would have to deal with the dream. Every night, Ryan would wake and spend hours trying to rid his mind of the beast that haunted his dreams. His parents had no idea the dream had returned, as Ryan would not call for his mother during the night like when he was younger. He would simply stare upward until his alarm would ring.

Ryan reached out and hit the button turning off his alarm. Stretching his arms high in the air, Ryan shuffled slowly across the floor, down the hallway to the bathroom. He slouched against the wall and slid to the floor as he waited for his sister to finish her turn in the bathroom.

Everything seemed to revolve around Shelly. She got to stay up later, be in the bathroom first and watch what she wanted on television. She could even be on the computer for hours, unsupervised. Shelly would take hours, primping and pampering herself, getting ready for another day of her wonderful life.

Ryan's family shared one bathroom. He was usually the last one in and had to rush to get ready.

Finally, Ryan got his turn. Shelly opened the bathroom door, and like a ghost floating through a fog, looked down and scoffed at Ryan as he lay on the hallway floor. He shrugged it off and slipped inside, closing the door behind him. Ryan turned on the shower, hoping to wake from the sluggish slumber of the morning.

Day after day, the same morning ritual...wake, wait in the hall, drag himself down the stairs after his shower, then waste as much time at the table, that is until his mother would force Ryan from the table and out the door in the direction of school. It wasn't always like this, however. Ryan used to like his walk to school, though he could barely remember such a time as he quickly made the journey down the tracks, through the alley and into the school building.

# 4

Ryan's trip to school used to be a blur. He would walk the three blocks, which included a set of train tracks that passed through town, a small candy store and then through an alley that lead straight to Lincoln Elementary. He barely noticed any of the distractions along the way.

There were no other students that lived in Ryan's building. Most of the people who lived there were older and their children had grown and moved away. This left Ryan no choice but to walk to school alone.

The first block was fine. Ryan would walk down the tracks, holding his arms straight out from his shoulders, pretending to be a high wire walker. Occasionally he would slip and have to catch his balance. Walking the tracks was, in a way, fun for Ryan. But there were strange men sitting along the tracks in an old abandoned rail car. Their faces were covered with long, thick beards and what wasn't covered with hair was covered with dirt. Ryan didn't pay them much attention and, likewise, they never bothered him.

The second block wasn't bad either. There were a few houses along that section of the walk and the next to the last house was Mr. Henry's. He had a dog that was a beast. It looked like something he had brought back from one of his trips to Alaska, like a wolf he caught and put on a leash. Ryan wanted to tell Mr. Henry to get a stronger chain because it was always breaking under the might of that animal, but he was too terrified to step one foot in his yard.

The last block was usually the best. There was a small candy store at the corner of the alley. Sometimes Ryan would find an old bottle that he could take into the store and exchange it for money. Not much money, but enough to buy a few pieces of candy. He would finish eating the candy as he walked through the alley just before getting to the school building. On this particular morning, Ryan could still see his breath in the alley even though the weather was getting warmer. The alley was always cold and dark, covered in shadow like a thick blanket. One thin beam of light fought its way through the darkness of the alley and produced just enough brightness for Ryan to make his way safely through.

Allegheny Manor was a large collection of apartment buildings adjacent to the candy store. They sat directly across the railroad tracks from the alley and the school building. This section of town was known to be very rough. Just like the alley, the sides of the buildings were covered in graffiti, with no brick left to its original color. Some days Ryan could smell fresh paint, as the superintendent would have The Manor's walls painted over with a light gray color. It didn't work. The newly painted walls seemed to attract more and more people to come and draw on them. Ryan thought it looked like a fresh canvas every time they painted the walls gray.

Something caught Ryan's eye this day. The flashing red and blue lights of a police car grabbed his attention. He witnessed an older boy being arrested for vandalizing one of the storefronts on Main Street. He watched as the police cuffed the boy's hands behind his back and were putting him in the back seat of the car, tucking in his head so that he didn't bump it on the roof. People everywhere were shouting obscenities as the boy was lowered into the car. Ryan was completely confused. The people were yelling at the police officers, not the criminal. He noticed that part of the front window of the candy store was covered by a large piece of plywood. The window had obviously been broken by someone. Baffled, Ryan turned from the insanity and headed in the direction of his school.

Ryan would not let anything distract him as he was focused on getting to school and reading books about Native Americans. Mrs. Engler, the school librarian, knew Ryan had an extraordinary interest in Native-

American tribes and communities. She decided to let him know that she had ordered and received three new books on the subject.

She also made a deal with Ryan. "I am willing to come to school early. There's so much work for me to do coming down to the end of the year. So many books to inventory, I will need to be here every day an hour early just to keep up with the workload. If your parents agree, you can come in early to read if you take at least one day per week and help re-shelve the books already in the computer. I have already gotten the 'okay' from Mrs. Elder, the principal. Take this permission slip home and have a parent sign it so they know exactly what we are going to do."

Ryan could hardly contain himself. He rushed home and burst through the front door. He was speaking so quickly, his mother at first thought he had gotten in trouble and was being punished.

"Slow down Ryan! Are you in trouble?" she asked.

"No, mom. I have an opportunity to get to school early, no other kids, no distractions, and read. You know how I love to read!"

Ryan's mother was caught a little off guard. "I knew you liked to read, but to go to school an extra hour per day...you must be really into books." She paused. "What are you reading?" she asked, actually very pleased in his enthusiasm for reading.

"A series on Native Americans. It's brand new!" Ryan answered.

"Yes," his mother said. "I believe we also ordered a series of books on Native- American culture. It's on back order and won't be here for another week or so."

"So, will you sign? I promise, Mother, I am going straight to school and ripping into those books!" Ryan finished. Although Mrs. Donaldson had no reason not to trust him, she did what any parent would do and called the school to confirm this arrangement. She was assured that it was on the "up-n-up" and signed the paper. Ryan was thrilled.

The first book entitled, "Through the Chief's Eyes" was on the importance of the "The Chief" He was the oldest and wisest man in the village and was a direct descendant of past chiefs. Any major decision that was made in the tribe couldn't and wouldn't be made without consulting him. Ryan was fascinated by the wisdom of the elder and the level of respect he received from the members of the tribe. He was also amazed by the process by which the tribe came to each decision. With any major decision, the counsel would be assembled and all facts and points of view would be heard. The decision was then based on what was in the best interest of the tribe. Individuality was taken out of the equation as the success of the tribe was more important than one individual. Ryan thought of his own situation and how different life would be if he were part of a tribe who thought of everyone, not just one or a few.

One morning, while he was reading, Ryan had completely forgotten about what time of day it was and sat quietly at the table. He heard a faint sound coming from the hallway. The bell to start the day! He was late to class. Ryan knew the consequences for being late. The first slip was just a warning. After two unexcused slips in one grading period, there would be a hearing with the teacher, principal and a parent to figure out why the student was tardy. And if a third slip were issued, there would be some sort of suspension.

Ryan explained to his teacher that he had been reading in the library since 7:00 a.m. He pleaded his case, but could not sway his teacher's opinion and received the first tardy slip for the grading period. Ryan apologized for being late and assured his teacher that it would not happen again. He took his seat and proceeded to take out his materials for math.

Try as he might during math class, he could not shake the book from his mind. He caught himself daydreaming about the villagers asking the Chief's advice about major decisions. He was quickly snapped back to reality when his teacher slammed her book on his desk, demanding he go to the board and complete the next math problem. Ryan jumped to his feet and shuffled to the board, doing as his teacher had asked. But he couldn't wait until class was over so that he could get back to that book.

Ryan quickly moved through the first book and was on to the second, "A Native Childhood" in no time. This book was about how each adult member of the tribe would spend time teaching the younger children the skills they would need to be successful members of the tribe. This read wasn't as interesting to Ryan. It was filled with facts about the functions of the tribe rather than interesting tales or stories of the past. Ryan felt less excited about this book, but when he finished, he was eager to get started on the third: From Boys to Men: The Trials of Manhood.

As night fell, Ryan was every excited knowing that when he woke in the morning, he would be able to return the second and get his hands on the third book of the series.

Ryan was awake, showered and out the door before his mother and sister were even out of bed. He raced down the tracks, avoiding some broken glass, sprinted past the dirty men standing in the boxcar cutting across the yard, and hurdled Mr. Henry's dog as it slept. He met Mrs. Engler at the door to the school and walked closely behind her, not wanting to waste a single second. He sat at the table with his feet tapping in anticipation.

Ryan read From Boys to Men for the better part of an

hour. He was completely absorbed. He imagined what life must have been like for these people. He closed his eyes and could actually see himself shooting a bow and arrow. Before Ryan knew it, the bell rang and snapped him out of the daydream. The bell to begin homeroom! Even though he had been to school before any other student (and half the teachers for that matter), he was late to homeroom again.

Ryan was sent to the office with his second tardy that month. Although Ryan had been at the school and was utilizing library books, the principal decided that he should not be allowed to come in early to read any longer because he could not get to his classroom on time.

Now those days seemed so long ago to Ryan. His walk to school was more of a chore than a means to the library and more books. The very next morning on his trip to school, Ryan noticed all the broken glass as he slipped off the tracks, landing on a broken bottle. Sharp pain raced through the side of his foot. Quickly he sat on the tracks, pulling his shoe and sock off to check out the damage. There was a small cut that barely broke the skin, not deep enough to bleed badly but just enough of a wound to cause some slight discomfort. Ryan slipped his sock and shoe over his throbbing foot. That's when, out of the corner of his eye, he noticed the strange men in the abandoned boxcar staring at him. Their stares made him very uncomfortable. All the while the wolf-like dog barked incessantly. Suddenly, Mr. Henry's dog broke its chain and chased him until Ryan slipped into the alley and hid behind a dumpster as the hound ran quickly past the entrance.

As Ryan peeked around the dumpster, he let out a long sigh of relief, realizing he had lost the hound. He stood, turned and headed through the alley on his way to school. He had only taken a few steps when he ran into something, or rather someone! He stared into the person's chest. Then he stumbled backward and slowly began to look up at the person's face.

Sammy Haggerton!

Ryan felt the knot in his stomach tighten...his palms sweaty. There stood Sammy, angrily glaring at him. Watching from around the corner was the meanest kid in the entire school. His name was Jake Farlow.

# 5

Jake was the most rotten kid in the 6th grade. According to rumors, he had failed a grade at his last school and even sent a boy to the hospital. Snapchat was a buzz with pictures and stories coming from the kids at Jake's last school. One story, Ryan thought was hard to believe, but many people said it was true. He heard that all the kid did was accidentally bump into Jake in the restroom and Jake let him have it. Jake grabbed him by the neck, pushed the kid headfirst into the urinal, resulting in a large cut above his eye that left him unconscious. There were never any charges brought against Jake because only two people knew what actually happened. Jake had threatened the boy, saying that if he said anything, Jake would surely track him down and finish what he started in the bathroom. Despite his small size, Jake was a truly intimidating figure.

From the moment he arrived at Lincoln Elementary, Jake was a troublemaker. During the first week of school, Jake had stolen one person's lunch and another kid's lunch money. Ryan was one of those unfortunate students.

Earlier that summer, looking at the class list that was posted online, Ryan's heart sank when he saw that he was in Mrs. Maslar's class. "Mrs. Maslar was a fantastic teacher, if you are an athlete," Ryan told his mother. "She favors the boys and girls who dominate at kickball or who can hit a Wiffle ball over the fence."

"Don't be ridiculous, Ryan!" his mother scolded him. "Mrs. Maslar is a professional. She sees every student as equal to ever other student."

Ryan shook his head back and forth. "Mom, you should see her at recess. I've watched her on the Sixth-Grade playground. She whips that ball when they are running the bases. I've seen her hit kids in the head and knock them head over heels!" Ryan went on. "She only high fives the kids who score or make a nice catch! I've never heard of her giving a boy or girl a fist bump or high five for getting a perfect score on a test or knocking it out of the park on a presentation. Now that would be professional," he concluded.

"You will have a good year with Mrs. Maslar," said his mother. "You'll see."

"Yeah, we'll see. The woman still wears her hair in a mullet! A mullet, mom! Bad enough some of the guys I've seen on the corner still think it's 1989, but a mullet on a woman, a teacher...really?"

Mrs. Donaldson was appalled.

"What an awful thing to say! You take that back right this instant, young man!" she demanded.

Ryan closed his eyes, knowing his words were hurtful.

"You're right, Mom. I shouldn't say those things. Maybe I will have a good year." He looked over the entire list. There were a few names he didn't recognize. Must be new students, Ryan thought.

On the first day of school, Mrs. Maslar made everyone in the Sixth-Grade play kickball. This did not please Ryan. He tried to hide in the outfield. Somewhere between center and right field was perfect. Three outs were made quickly, and Ryan's team was up to kick. The team captain, Joey Bowser had a plan. He wanted a girl to go first, not just any girl however, Jenny Terwint, the best athlete in the grade. Jenny blasted a line drive shot into the outfield and made it safely to first base. With no outs, Joey wanted Ryan to kick second. He wanted to get Ryan out of the way so the better players could kick the ball and Jenny would score a run. Much to his surprise, and everyone else's, on his first time up, Ryan kicked the ball toward third base on the third pitch from Mrs. Maslar. The first pitch Ryan kicked with all his might, but somehow missed the ball completely. The second attempt, he nudged the ball foul down the first base line. Players on the other team yelled and moved in toward him.

But the third time was the charm! Jenny stood, hands on hips, as she expected the ball to roll foul, again. Samson Riggley, the kid with the strongest arm in the school, raced forward and picked the ball up before it could roll foul. Jenny's eyes bulged as she realized she needed to run. She took off toward second base. Samson delivered a perfect throw to second base to get Jenny out. Ryan was so shocked that he stood and watched the ball roll toward third base. "RUN!" All his teammates screamed. Arms and legs flailing, Ryan began to run. When he got to first base, he realized what it felt like to be "safe". He couldn't believe it!

His excitement lasted only long enough for Mrs. Maslar to roll the next pitch. With two outs, Joey told Ryan to run as soon as the ball was kicked. As soon as it was kicked, Ryan took off toward second base, never looking to where the ball was actually headed. The ball rolled directly to Mrs. Maslar. Instead of lobbing the ball to get the easy out at second base, she took one step in Ryan's direction and unleashed a bullet. The ball caught Ryan in the lead foot and, like a strike in bowling, knocked both feet out from under him.

Ryan came crashing down with a thud. Everyone laughed, including Mrs. Maslar. "You should've jumped!" she yelled to him. Ryan's teammates even made fun of him. He concluded that he was much better off staying by himself and reading. He hoped that he wouldn't be forced to play kickball ever again. From that point on, Mrs. Maslar didn't force the kids to play. Only the kids who really were competitive played with her. On nice days, Ryan would head to the picnic area of the playground and read. He didn't speak to or bother anyone.

Jake had spotted Ryan immediately. He was very observant and recognized right away that Ryan had no close friends. He saw Ryan as the perfect target, a victim. Jake also had a keen eye for spotting potential threats. He quickly made his presence known to all in the Sixth- Grade.

Vincent Imbragnito and Sammy Haggerton could have made big trouble for Jake, had they banned together against him. The two were at least a head taller than Jake and outweighed him by twenty pounds each. These boys were mountains with huge bodies and little brains. Thin mustaches shaded their upper lips. Sammy had been held back a year when he was in kindergarten, and Vince was suspended for a year and had to take summer school just to pass the Fifth Grade and head into Sixth. Vince had hardly come to school the entire year before. His mother was taken to the district magistrate because of his truancy. He would hang out all day long at the apartment buildings right next to the school.

In Third Grade, there was a boy who always wore what looked to the kids like a bike helmet. His name was Kyle. Most of the boys, including Ryan, felt sorry for him. A rumor floated among the kids that Kyle had a soft spot on the top of his head and needed to wear the helmet to protect it. Vince saw the helmet as a target. Vince always hit Kyle on top of the helmet, swinging his arm as hard as he could and clobbering the poor kid. Kyle couldn't do anything to defend himself. He couldn't communicate very well to the teachers either. They surely would have stopped this from happening, had they known. There were no students who would turn Vince or Sammy in for the mean things they did. Most thought that it was better to be a quiet witness than a suffering victim.

That Sixth-Grade year would be forever changed after Jake's arrival. At first, he appeared to be harmless. Jake wasn't much taller than Ryan, but what he lacked in size, he made up for in darkness and cruelty. Nothing seemed to be inside when Jake would stare someone down with an expressionless face, cold and dark.

On the Friday of his first week in Sixth-Grade, Ryan walked into the restroom just outside the cafeteria doors. He was usually one of the last to leave the lunchroom. He would wait until everyone was out of the restroom before entering. Ryan never used the urinals in the restroom. He felt uncomfortable and self-conscious standing near the other boys so he locked himself in a stall and went about his business. Sitting quietly, Ryan heard footsteps enter the restroom. He slowly, quietly picked his feet off the floor to avoid being seen. The footsteps got closer and he saw a shadow walk by his door. Peeking between a crack in the wall and the stall door, Ryan saw it was Jake. He tried not to breathe, as he didn't want Jake to know he was there. More footsteps! Shadows passed quickly by the crack.

"New kid, huh!" It was more of a statement, not a question. Ryan heard the words coming from one of the boys, Sammy. Ryan could now see three boys' reflections in the mirror, through the crack. Sammy and Vince surrounded Jake, who didn't break a sweat.

"Yep, I'm the new kid," he said, as if he knew they would come after him and lured them into the bathroom.

"This is how we do things 'round here," said Vince. But before Sammy could utter a single word, Jake slammed his fist into Vince's stomach, just below his breastbone. And in the opposite motion with the same arm, he dropped Sammy with the fastest and most vicious elbow Ryan had ever seen thrown. Both boys collapsed on the bathroom floor. Ryan at first felt relief as Jake had taken down the two biggest bullies at Lincoln Elementary. The thought quickly vanished as he watched Jake kneel down over the two boys as they gasped for air.

"Don't worry," Jake said. "The air will return to your lungs in a few minutes." It was the most frightening voice Ryan had ever heard, lacking all emotion. Jake sounded like he couldn't care less if the two boys ever got their wind back and passed out right there on the restroom floor.

"I am running the show from now on, got it?" Jake whispered as cold as ever. "You two will do whatever I say, whenever I say it. Won't you?" Both boys shook their heads yes, still trying to catch their breaths.

"Good, so we understand each other," Jake said as he walked out the door, leaving the duo lying helplessly on the cold bathroom tile. Jake looked toward the direction of the bathroom stall where Ryan was hiding. His eye squinted and he walked away.

Ryan couldn't believe what he had just witnessed. The new kid, outnumbered and greatly undersized, taking out the two biggest bullies in the school. It was planned, all calculated. Ryan realized just then that even though Jake wasn't the biggest or strongest boy in the grade, he was the meanest and most cunning. He knew that Jake had to be avoided at all costs.

Being aware of all three boys would consume most of Ryan's thoughts. He tried to steer clear of most kids who were known as troublemakers.

He was always more comfortable doing things by himself. He didn't want help. He didn't need help. Ryan was sure he could get through life all by himself. But the school guidance counselor tried to convince Ryan that there was "safety in numbers."

One day when the teachers were able to choose a student from their classroom to eat lunch with the school counselor, Ryan's name was chosen. Ms. Scarlota knew that Ryan was a loner and wanted to help him have the best Sixth-Grade experience a kid could have. At least that's what the poster plastered on her office door read.

Ryan knocked and opened the door to her office. "Come in, Ryan! Close the door!" Ms. Scarlota said, her voice so high pitched that Ryan thought only a dog could hear it.

"Ryan," Ms. Scarlota began, "have you ever watched any of the shows on cable television about life on the Serengeti?"

Ryan's face wrinkled, one eyebrow up and the other almost closed upon his eye. "Umm, no?" he answered. "Ms. Scarlota, what does this have to do with me?"

"Here" she said, "sit and let me show you what I mean." The small, red-haired Ms. Scarlota walked to her desk. Walked was more of an overstatement. She shuffled, wearing one of her long dresses with huge high heels. The kids at school thought she never lifted her feet more than an inch for fear of stepping on her skirt and tripping herself. Ms. Scarlota opened the drawer and pulled out a VHS tape entitled, Africa.

VHS tape, Ryan thought. Now she is really showing

her age. Nobody has tapes anymore.

Ms. Scarlota shuffled across the floor and placed the tape in the VCR. The television crackled. Ryan imagined he saw sparks fly and smoke rise from the back. He looked around to see if he was being "punked." He thought this couldn't be happening.

The picture on the television set rolled from top to bottom a few seconds and then settled. "Life on the Serengeti..." the tape began. Soon lions were on the prowl. Herds of wildebeests trampled across the scorched earth. The camera zoomed in on one lonely animal. The lions had it surrounded. Suddenly, a lion that had been crouching in the tall grass sprang into action, grabbing the young wildebeest by the throat.

Ryan jumped back in his seat, stunned at what he had just seen. Ms. Scarlota shut the TV off. "Do you see what I mean?" she asked. "There is safety in numbers."

He nodded his head yes and quickly left the room. Walking down the hall, he began to think about what had just happened.

Ryan concluded that she meant if he had a friend or two "to hang around with," as she once put it, he would be a little safer. He guessed Ms. Scarlota was talking about his walk to school and the dangers it posed.

She knew nothing about the troubles with Sammy and the others. She didn't know how it felt to turn the corner and enter the alley. Ms. Scarlota couldn't know how Ryan trembled at the mere thought of the daily abuse. Ryan knew what had happened to him when he was at daycare. He learned that tattling to a teacher or counselor only got you into more trouble. Besides, this was outside of school.

Ryan's heart pounded and he began to sweat just at the thought of telling on Sam and Vince. He couldn't imagine what evil torture they would impose on him. So he did what any smart kid would do. Ryan stayed quiet, kept his head down and kept to himself.

Ryan was fortunate that his mother worked at the town library. Over the weekend, he was able to sign out a similar book to the one he had been reading at school. The following Monday, he sat quietly turning the pages. Jake spotted Ryan sitting alone, quietly reading. He turned to Vince and said, "What a GEEK! Do you see that kid read'n?" he asked disgustingly.

"Yeah, what a nerd!" Vincent replied.

"Let's go educate him on the rules of playground etiquette," sneered Jake.

"Etiquette," Vince repeated, pretending to know what the word meant.

Jake moved in first, snatching the book from Ryan's hand. He didn't stand a chance. The picnic tables were just out of sight from where the teachers sat during recess. Three smaller kids were also sitting at the table. With only a quick glance and a glare, the table was cleared, the three youngsters disappearing into the crowd of students playing tag. Not one went to get Ryan any help, even though they knew what was going to happen to him. Ryan was left to his own devices.

"Indians, huh?" Jake said with a sneer, looking at Ryan's book. "What's wrong with you? Why don't you join us on the playground for a little fun?"

"Yeah, fun!" Sammy and Vince said simultaneously as they surrounded Ryan.

"Well, I was just sitting here, minding my own business, reading about..." Ryan's voice was shaky and cut off by Jake.

"Enjoying a book? How could you enjoy a book about savages, especially during recess?" snapped Jake. "Wait, I know you..."

"You do?" Ryan asked.

Jake leaned in closely. "I know you were in the stall the other day," he whispered to Ryan.

Ryan's eyes widened in disbelief. "I wasn't bothering anyone or..."

"Quiet, Indian boy!" Jake demanded. "This is how things are going to be. You're going to give me your lunch. I don't have one and I'm starving."

"But I noticed you took that kid's lunch." Ryan pointed across the playground at another student. "Besides, I didn't pack. I'm buying."

"That's where you're wrong!" answered Jake. "I'm

going to buy, using your money and you're going to like it!" Jake squeezed Ryan's shoulder. "And here's the best part," Jake said with a sarcastic chuckle. "You won't say a word of this to anyone, right?" Jake increased the pressure on Ryan's shoulder. Ryan didn't answer.

"RIGHT!" Jake pressed his face against Ryan's. The boys were nose to nose. Ryan was terrified. Jake's face was pale and his eyes were cold and dark.

"Okay," Ryan said sheepishly, looking at the ground, as he didn't want to stare directly into Jake's eyes again. He reached into his pocket and gave Jake the money.

Just then the bell rang to end recess. All the students rushed to the entrance and began to file back into the building. All but Ryan, Jake, Sammy and Vince. When Ryan stood, Jake stopped and turned toward him, handing him back his book.

"No hard feelin's, Indian Boy!" said Jake.

"No," replied Ryan. Just as the words were falling from his lips, Jake shoved him backwards. Without knowing it, Vince had knelt behind Ryan and when Jake shoved him, Ryan was sent head over heels, with the back of his head landing against the gravel underneath the picnic table.

"Later, Sacagawea!" one of the boys yelled as they ran toward the entrance.

For a moment, Ryan was dizzy. Tears filled his eyes as he lay on the ground staring at the clear blue sky. His head began to throb.

Ryan picked himself off the ground and made his way into the building, rubbing the back of his head. His teacher, Mrs. Maslar, noticed the back of his shirt was grass-stained and asked him what had happened. Ryan put his dead down and pretended not to hear her. She stopped him and asked again. He quickly concocted a story about tripping over the bench. He was carrying his book and didn't want to damage it as he fell, so he rolled onto his back. He bumped his head and made himself dizzy. She told him to go to the restroom and get himself together before returning to class.

This kind of treatment was not an everyday occurrence for Ryan. That was part of the problem. He never felt safe during recess even when nothing happened. Jake was always in the back of his mind. He never knew where or when a confrontation would happen.

Jake didn't fall into the regular category of a "bully." In the past, kids known as bullies would play hooky for days at a time. Not Jake. He rarely missed a day. Ryan thought he saw flashes of Jake actually enjoying himself at school but would NEVER say anything to him. That would just instigate another beating and Ryan did not want that. If he could, Ryan would avoid Jake at all costs.

In the beginning, the harassment was contained to recess only. Ryan usually felt safe walking to and from school. The usual distractions he could handle. Something big changed for Ryan, however, and he never saw it coming.

One day as Ryan was reading during recess, Jake appeared and demanded more money for the next day. What Jake didn't realize was that the teachers had begun to walk around the playground area because the weather had been so warm that spring day. Jake, clinched Ryan by the shirt, choking him, and demanded that in the future Ryan bring more money with him to school.

"I want to get juice with my lunch from now on! I'm sick of drinking milk!" Jake shouted. Ryan, looking over Jake's shoulder, could see the teachers walking in their direction and snapped back at Jake.

"You're not getting a penny out of me!" said Ryan.

Jake was furious. He reached back his right arm, made a fist and was ready to strike Ryan down.

"Jake, what is going on here?" Mrs. Maslar asked.

Jake let go of Ryan and straightened his shirt.

"Oh, nothing," said Jake. "We were just talking about what was for lunch today," Jake glared at Ryan.

For the rest of the day, Jake never let Ryan out of his sight. He even followed Ryan home. Ryan had no idea Jake was there as the other boy kept his distance. Jake made mental notes about Ryan's trip to school. That evening he plotted and planned. He realized the perfect place to pin Ryan down was in the alley.

Jake walked to Sammy's place and sat on the stoop outside. "Go into the alley," Jake told Sam. "Wait until you hear him coming. Step out and impede his progress."

Sam squinted and Jake knew he didn't understand the directions.

"Stand along the wall in the shadows. He'll never see you. Step out and get in his way." Jake rolled his eyes and repeated himself in a way that Sam could follow.

"You want me to give him the business, huh?" Sam asked, pounding his fist into his hand.

"No, not yet." Jake paused. "I just want to know how he will react to someone else being in the alley."

The next morning, Sam followed his orders. He was up early and waiting in the shadows of the alley. After racing to outrun Mr. Henry's dog and hiding behind the dumpster to make sure the dog was gone, Ryan quickly turned to dart his way out of the alley when he ran smack into Sammy.

He stared into his chest, then directly into his face. He stumbled backward. Sammy didn't say a word. He just stared at Ryan with squinted eyes. Ryan was able to make his way around the mountain of a kid and quickly bolted into the building. As he scurried past, Sammy turned his head and then slowly closed his eyes, as if knowing what would happen to Ryan in the future. That day during lunch Ryan noticed that Sammy, Vince and Jake were whispering and looking in his direction.

Their stares made Ryan very uncomfortable. He tried to ignore them and continued to read, but he could feel the weight of their stares as they grinned villainously. Ryan was nervous. He was sure something bad would happen, but nothing did. He sat and tried to read but was looking about the playground the entire time.

The next morning, a warm breeze blew through Ryan's hair as the sun warmed his face. Ryan tilted his head back and took a deep breath, smelling the fresh spring air. The morning walk to school was filled with the sounds of tiny warblers and English sparrows that had returned for spring. A bright red male cardinal caught his attention as it sang loudly for all to hear. Ryan found an old Coke bottle in perfect condition along the tracks. He raced into the corner store and exchanged the bottle for a few pieces of candy. He opened the wrapper and chewed the first piece as he made his way to the alley. The pink colored candy melted in his mouth, helping him to forget about the darkness of the alley, at least for a moment.

Ryan always became a bit nervous walking through the alley because it was permanently cold and dark. He passed the large dumpster that sat alongside of the building half way through the alley. He caught a glimpse of someone standing at the rear of the dumpster. Ryan kept his head down and picked up his pace.

Out of fear, Ryan did not lift his head to see where

he was going and slammed into Sammy and Vince. He tried to look past them and see just how far it was to the end of the alley. Maybe he could make a run for it. He was so close to the end but was trapped. Then the boy from behind the dumpster spoke.

"We've been waiting for you, Ryan," Jake said in a low and terrifying voice. He stepped out and stood behind Ryan and closed off any chance of escape. The one thin beam of light landed square on Jake's face. Ryan was completely surrounded.

Jake ripped Ryan's bag from his hand. Ryan quietly asked, "What do you want with me?"

"Do you think I forgot about your little stunt the other day?" Jake asked sarcastically. "Not so sassy when the teachers aren't around, are ya?" he continued. "You know what I want! Your money!"

Ryan reached into his pocket and pulled out the $1.25 he would use for his lunch later that day. He held out his hand. Jake quickly snatched up the money.

"What am I to do for lunch now?" Ryan asked.

"Don't know, don't care!" replied Jake. "That's not my problem!"

As the two boys were talking, Sammy and Vince rifled through Ryan's bag taking an mp3 player and a cell phone. Ryan couldn't do anything to save his possessions. As all three boys ran off in the direction of the school, Ryan was left in the alley, helpless. He had been outnumbered.

From that moment on, Ryan decided to leave all his possessions at home. He took only the essentials to school. Ryan's family was not wealthy by any means, but they weren't poor either. His father insisted Ryan get a job the summer before his Sixth-Grade year. He wanted Ryan to understand the value of hard work. Just after his twelfth birthday, Ryan was fortunate. He saw a flier posted on the bulletin board at the library where his mother worked for a local newspaper delivery boy. The papers would be delivered between 3 p.m. and 5 p.m. every afternoon.

Ryan read the advertisement and called the phone number at the bottom. A very rough, sharp voice answered.

"Hello!" The voice barked.

"Hi, my name is Ryan. I am calling about the delivery position," Ryan quietly said.

"You're hired!" the voiced barked again. "Come pick up your bag every Tuesday and Thursday afternoon. Return the bag each afternoon when you finish."

Ryan was confused. "That's it?" he asked. "You don't want to ask me any questions?"

"No!" the man said sharply. "You can fill out the paperwork when you pick up your bag of papers. So be here early!" He slammed the phone down before Ryan could respond. He was even more confused. He didn't know where to go or what to do. He searched the flier and found an address printed in the lower left-hand corner.

Ryan was pleased that he had gotten a job. He smiled as he navigated his way downtown, dodging quickly moving cars and fast-talking people.

He knocked on the door. It opened quickly with such force it almost sucked Ryan inside.

"You Ryan?" It was the same rough voice as the phone.

"Yes," Ryan replied. He looked up at the towering figure standing before him. His hair was a salt and pepper mix, cut short on the sides and high and tight on top. His mustache was the same as his hair, thick and completely hiding his upper lip. His eyes bulged.

"You sure?" the man said. "You need to be at least 12 years old to do this job! Did you even read the flyer?"

"Yes Sir, I read it and I am of age," Ryan said confidently for the first time in his life.

The man grunted. "We'll see. Here, fill this out and return it when you return the bag. Make sure you get a parent's signature too." He shoved the paper at Ryan and slammed the door shut.

Ryan grabbed the bag and the list of streets he was to cover. He was on his way to making money. Not much money, mind you, but enough to buy books at the book fair and supplies he wanted for school.

Delivering the papers was fun for Ryan. It got him up and moving. Throughout summer and fall, rain or shine, he was on his bike tossing papers into the yards of his neighbors. During the winters, the papers would be delivered on foot. The routes were cut from six streets to just three to enable the deliverers to ensure customers got their papers before five o'clock. Ryan had worked for the paper for a year now and had money saved in his room.

He bought cool pens that would light up when you were writing. Others had many different colors of ink. Ryan had the neatest tablets, some with super heroes and some with scenes of mountains on the cover. He had pencils with different thicknesses of lead. Some clicked, others twisted. Now even these items weren't safe.

Soon the hoodlums were taking the pens and pencils that Ryan had purchased with his own money. He had folders and binders that were destroyed for no other reason than Ryan didn't have anything else for them to take. Nothing of Ryan's was safe! He was forced to borrow pencils from the teacher. These Ryan did not like. Every time he had to sharpen one, the lead was broken on the inside and when he would return to his seat and touch the pencil to his paper, the lead would fall right out. He would have to repeat the scenario all over again. Sometimes the pencils would be completely lopsided. On one side the lead would be completely exposed, while on the other the wood went clear to the end, rendering the pencil useless. When he was tired of laboring with these useless pencils, he went to his teacher.

When Ryan had nothing else for the bullies to take or destroy, they began knocking him around. They would surround Ryan, pushing and pulling at him, calling him names and kicking him to the ground.

Unlike the treatment at recess, the meeting in the alley happened every day. Where Ryan's home was located, following the train tracks and walking through the alley was the most direct route to school. If he were to walk the next block past the alley to avoid the trouble awaiting there, Ryan knew he would be exposing himself to something even worse. Just past the elementary school was the section of town that both of Ryan's parents warned him to stay away from. They explained to him that he would be putting himself into grave danger by walking into that neighborhood so he steered clear of that part of town. This left Ryan to walk the tracks and scurry through the alley.

Sometimes Sammy and Vince wouldn't be there, but Jake always was. Every morning walk to school, Ryan knew he would face the meanest bully to ever walk the halls of Lincoln Elementary. Everyday Ryan went hungry while Jake ate well.

One day Ryan had a brilliant idea. Because of the paper route, Ryan had money. He was very proud of the fact that he told his parents that he could pay for his own lunches at school. Several small jars were filled with lose change sitting on his dresser. Ryan had dollar bills stashed away in his underwear drawer. He dipped into this cache of money and secretly placed the extra $1.25 into his sock. When Jake confronted him, he handed over the money, all the while knowing that he would use the money in his sock to get lunch. If Ryan had money for Jake, he still took a little abuse from the boys, but was then left to go on his way.

Later that same day, Ryan used the extra money to buy a lunch. He went to a far-off corner where nobody sat and peacefully ate. He ate a huge slice of deep-dish pizza and a mixed fruit cocktail while drinking chocolate milk. When he finished he had such a strong feeling of accomplishment that he had actually outsmarted Jake. He leaned back in his chair confidently. He also felt something he hadn't felt at school in a long time—full. His stomach was nearly bursting.

One day at lunch, Jake was told by the lunch monitor to get a mop from the corner closet. The monitor didn't actually see Jake trip the fifth grader who had fallen and spilled his tray of food all over the cafeteria floor, but he did have a very strong suspicion that Jake was the culprit based on the laughing and carrying on at the bully's table. But the only thing the monitor could do was to make Jake get a mop and help the younger boy clean up the mess. Jake argued his case.

"I didn't do anything!" he shouted. "Why do I have to clean it up?" Before the monitor could answer, Jake turned and stomped away in the direction of the closet where the mops and cleaning supplies were kept.

Jake, mumbling obscenities, walked past the table where Ryan sat. He glanced down to see who would sit so far away from the rest of the cafeteria. He was amazed! He looked down and saw Ryan had eaten a school lunch. Jake realized that he had been deceived. Jake was furious but kept it to himself. He opened the closet door and got the mop. He even cleaned up the entire mess himself.

"Look out!" Jake shouted at the fifth grader. "You are making it worse." He grabbed the mop from the boy and shoved him backwards. Jake proceeded to work. He was so focused on Ryan that he hadn't realized that he had actually done a good deed by cleaning everything.

The day went on without a glitch for Ryan. He wasn't bothered at recess and actually felt good about the day. He returned home and went straight to his room and recorded everything in his journal. He wrote about the discussion he had with his social studies teacher about the Indians who lived in this region before the Pilgrims arrived. He even mentioned in his journal that Jake and the others had left him alone that day. He wrote, "Today was a great day! Things may be turning around for me! As long as Jake had his money, and I hid the extra lunch money, things are good! Jake and the others left me alone and I got to eat!" He was feeling pretty confident that maybe things would be different from now on.

Again Ryan was chased by the huge wolf-like creature that Mr. Henry called a dog as he slipped into the alley and hid behind the dumpster. With his heart pounding and chest heaving, trying to catch his breath, he heard what sounded like a small piece of gravel being kicked across the pavement. The pebble rolled and stopped right at Ryan's feet. He looked up and stared directly into Jake's stone-cold face.

"You know the drill, Tonto!" Jake said.

Ryan obediently pulled the $1.25 from his pocket and handed it to Jake. He took a few steps to get by the boys but was grabbed and held tight.

"That's not enough today!" Jake shouted.

While Sammy and Vince held onto to Ryan, Jake rummaged through each of Ryan's pockets looking for more money but found nothing.

This enraged Jake! He slugged Ryan in the stomach, knocking him to the ground. Still Ryan kept quiet. He saw Jake roll over a cement block and pick something off the ground. Jake showed Sammy and Vince the fat and juicy worm he found. Ryan struggled to get to his feet, only to be kicked back to the ground. Jake ordered Vince to grab Ryan. Vince pulled Ryan to his feet by his hair. He grabbed Ryan's arm and lifted it behind his back. When the pressure was too much, Ryan screamed in pain. With his mouth open, Jake slammed the giant night crawler inside. Ryan almost puked. Quickly he tried to spit the worm out, but Jake had covered his mouth.

"Chew and swallow!" Jake demanded. "Chew and swallow now!"

Tears streamed down Ryan's face as he did what he was told. He chewed and swallowed.

Jake then cracked Ryan across the cheek with the back of his hand, sending Ryan spinning and falling back to the ground.

"You don't hand over all your money, this is what will happen from now on, GOT IT?" yelled Jake. All the while, the others were chanting, "Cry Baby, Cry Baby."

They all sprinted out of the alley and headed toward the school. Ryan could hear them as they laughed and called him names while they ran.

Ryan, on his hand and knees, began to puke. The worm wouldn't stay down, nor did he want it to. He wiped the tears from his face and with every ounce of energy he could muster, Ryan dragged himself, limping, the rest of the way to school.

Ryan's hair was a mess. There was a dirty abrasion

on his left cheek. His shirt that was usually tucked in neatly was half out on his right hip and covered in mud. Mrs. Maslar looked up as he entered the room. Her eyes widened. "Ryan, are you okay? What happened to you?" She was very concerned. Ryan scanned the back of the room and made eye contact with Jake. The bully, slouched in his chair, glared back, hoping the intimidation would be enough to keep Ryan quiet.

"Did you hear me, Ryan? Are you okay?" Mrs. Maslar repeated.

Ryan told his teacher a tall tale about trying to break his own record of getting to school. He told her that he was crossing the tracks and stumbled. He fell face first into the dirt and gravel. Mrs. Maslar accepted this excuse and instructed him to be more careful walking to school next time.

Jake leaned back in his chair, feeling confident that Ryan would not turn him in.

Ryan's teacher wasn't the only one to notice his appearance. Ryan's mother started to ask him where most of his things, his iPod and phone, were. He told her that his new friend, Jake, was playing with them at school. Mrs. Donaldson was fooled. She seemed happy he was making friends.

What was Ryan to do? Every night, he didn't want to go to bed for more reasons than he wanted to think about. Not only would morning arrive quickly, but once he fell asleep he had to face the recurring nightmare. He was tormented on a nightly basis by the same dream. An enormous grizzly stalking him, paw raised and ready to strike.

# 6

Now that Ryan wasn't able to come early to the school library, he spent all his spare time in the JFK Memorial Library, where his mother worked. Although she would encourage him to go outside and play on such nice spring Saturdays, he refused. He knew that somewhere out there Jake loomed. He was victim enough during the week. Why would he want to be beaten up on the weekends, too? Ryan lived for Saturday and Sunday.

After doing some research at his mother's library, he found the book he was reading at school, From Boys to Men: The Trials of Manhood.

The book dealt with the rough life of a Native-American boy. Before his 13th birthday, to become a man and find his place in the tribe, a boy must pass the ultimate test. He must live for an entire year having no contact with the tribe.

Ryan was fascinated around how these people would send boys on a journey apart from the tribe for an entire year. Each boy must fend for himself, having no interaction with anyone from the tribe through four seasons. How harsh and lonely a time this must have been, Ryan thought. This time was called the Seasons Away.

The entire year before being sent out to fend for himself, each boy would be taught all he would need to know about survival. Making a bow, arrows and arrowheads, tracking and hunting animals and preparing and preserving food and clothing would be essential to know to make it through this rough time.

When the time would finally arrive, the young boy would build a sweat lodge and spend twenty-four hours inside. The boy's father would enter the lodge only to pour water over the hot rocks surrounding the fire. This would fill the lodge with a tremendous heat. After spending twenty-four hours straight inside the lodge with no food or water, the boy would emerge and report to the chief. Everything the boy saw or experienced while in the lodge would be told to the chief. He would determine what each of the signs meant.

Many boys would see an animal during their time in the sweat lodge. The chief would explain to the boy that the animal would watch over him during the Seasons Away. Not all boys, Ryan read, saw an animal that would protect them. These boys would most likely have trouble away from the tribe.

The most important aspect of the Seasons Away was

for a boy to find a place to live. It had to be close to water, but not along the feeding paths of a grizzly bear, mountain lion or any other predator. The water was important not only for drinking but also for taking fish to eat and keeping any plants, such as corn, watered over the summer.

Every boy would be taught all they would need to know to survive. Each member of the family would teach the boys something different. Mothers, fathers, uncles and grandfathers would be their instructors. The day would be split into four distinct learning times.

The first part of the day, the mother would spend much of the time teaching her son how to plant food and when to harvest. She would also lecture him on the importance of preserving the crops and any meat that was taken. Nuts and berries could be picked and then set out to dry. Once dried of all moisture, they could be put into a small pouch and kept for a snack. This food would help to ensure that sustenance was available to keep the boys energized and healthy. Preparing clothing was also very important.

When all information was passed on about food preparation and storage, the mother would then teach the boy how to stretch the hides of the animals to dry. These skins would be very important when the weather would turn cold. She would explain how to turn these skins into articles of clothing. Moccasins, blankets and shawls would keep anyone warm and dry deep into the long cold winter. In the existence of the tribe, this type of work was considered to be women's work, to be done only by the squaws in the village. However, the boys would not be able to rely on a squaw to do this work during the trials, so it would be essential for them to learn how to plant and tend a small garden, make clothes and prepare food. The first lesson would take the boy most of the morning to learn.

The boy's uncle would take the portion of time directly after the midday meal. He would teach his nephew how to hunt and trap. Tracking was very important to taking prey.

First, looking at tracks left in the dirt would let anyone know where the animal was, when it was there and the direction in which it was heading.

Indian folk also had to be aware of... being hunted. Left alone in the wild, the young boys would be vulnerable to attack. The biggest and most feared predator was the great grizzly bear. Among the Indians, it was well known that once a grizzly tasted human blood, that was the only thing it would crave. Knowing this would make the hunter aware that he might be the hunted. Once aware, he could defend himself as necessary.

The best places to set traps were on heavily used trails and along the creek banks. These spots were also the best places to set up ambush hunts, when predators would hide close to paths or water holes. When the animal or prey would walk closely by, it would be taken by surprise, overwhelmed and killed. That is when the work would truly begin. Every ounce of the animal would be used. The meat would be prepared, the skin dried for clothing, the bones used for tools and even the insides used for a thread-like material. Nothing would go to waste.

Next, the boy's father would spend hours teaching him how to fashion a bow and arrows made from the ash tree.

The most important piece of equipment to accompany the bow and arrow was the arrowhead, made from a thin flat rock carved into razor sharp piercing points. Once attached to the arrow, it became a very valuable weapon. But making an arrowhead would take many lessons to master.

The boy's grandfather interested Ryan the most. He had never met his own grandfather, so this section grabbed and held his attention. He wondered what information his grandfather would have passed to him, or what he may have learned had the two ever met. Ryan had asked his father several times about his grandfather, but his dad would never answer. The subject would always be changed or the question would be ignored altogether.

In the book, Ryan learned the grandfather would

pass on the memories and tales of past boys and their experiences during their Seasons Away. He would also teach about the powerful bond between man and spirit. The Native American culture believed that animals were born with the spirits of their ancestors, and the boys were to respect and honor those spirits that have offered themselves to be taken. After every kill, "thanks" must be given in the way of a chant or song the hunter would sing. This song would thank the spirit of the animal for giving itself to the hunter.

The grandfather would also explain dreams, or "visions." These would sometimes come to a young boy while he slept. Sometimes it would be a picture of the past that in some way would help guide that person's future. Some of the boys could have already had a vision but had no idea what it meant until the grandfather would explain in great detail why the dream occurred.

This part of the teaching somewhat confused Ryan. He always looked at dreams as just thoughts during sleep. He never thought that his dreams could in some way be trying to tell him what to do. Now he began to think about dreams he had in the past and what they meant or how they might guide his future. Ryan began to think more deeply about the bear in his dream.

His mind shifted and he began to remember a dream he recently had about the upcoming Sixth-Grade project. He had a dream that he was standing before the class speaking in a Native-American tongue and showing them how to make an arrowhead. If this was a 'vision', how would that guide my future? he thought. His mind then shifted once again to the Sixth-Grade project itself.

As a Sixth-Grade graduation project, students were to choose a topic, research it and present the information before the entire class. Ryan knew immediately what his project would be—Native Americans. He chose the particular ritual about the trials and tribulations of the Seasons Away. Still many other aspects of their way of life intrigued him.

Ryan was in the library every spare moment he had. He also spent hours looking up information on the Internet. One article in particular caught Ryan's attention—shape shifting. Ryan read that shape shifting occurred throughout native cultures via songs, dances and life. Dancers wore feathers or hides of animals and performed dances using the motions of the animal they were imitating. This action would strengthen the bond between themselves and the animal spirits that surround them. Sometimes a young boy would study an animal so closely and imitate it so well, others would believe the boy could in some ways become that animal. The entire culture was so closely tied to the life around it and to the earth itself that its people were thought of as part of the animal kingdom. They did not look at their surroundings as if they were any better than the life that revolved around them.

The project consumed his every thought. He was so focused and intent on delivering the best presentation, he didn't mind coughing up money to Jake on a daily basis. On the day of the presentation, Ryan was ready.

The report was four pages long, using illustrations and even some artifacts donated by the library for the project. Ryan didn't even need the note cards he had made. He rattled off the information as if he had lived through the Seasons Away himself. Pauwan, one of the native languages that intrigued him began to flow from his tongue. Ryan caught himself speaking this way and became nervous. He paused for what seemed like hours. He then explained to the class what some of the words had meant and how they were used. This pulled his class into the presentation all the more.

His eyes scanned the audience to see their reaction. Most of the students were literally on the edge of their seats. They were deathly still, leaning forward and hanging on every word Ryan spoke. Everything was quiet. Ryan began to sweat but continued with his presentation.

When Ryan finished the class stood and cheered. Some were even whistling, all but Jake. He sat in the back glaring at Ryan. He couldn't stand that Ryan had this attention.

Mrs. Maslar seemed fascinated by the report and the depth of Ryan's explanations. She couldn't believe he knew how to speak the language and what the words meant.

Finally, something I can feel good about again at school, Ryan thought to himself as the students came to the front of the class to congratulate him. From behind, Ryan felt two study hands grasp his shoulders. His body lurched forward and back. He was frightened at first then he heard Mrs. Maslar say, "Ryan, that was fantastic!" She raised her right hand, "C'mon, don't leave me hangin'!"

Ryan reached up and swung with all his might. SMACK! Hands collided! A stinging sensation pulsed through his hand.

"Alright!" Mrs. Maslar said, strutting back to her desk. "Now that's what I'm talking about! That's how you give a presentation!" she announced to the class.

Ryan answered questions from his classmates for thirty minutes and even showed them how the Indians transformed a simple flat rock into an arrowhead. As he was creating the arrowhead, he stopped and realized this was exactly like the dream he had. The entire presentation he gave was familiar to him, not because he had done all the research, but from the dream he had.

Everything was the same...the presentation, the

questions and the making of the arrowhead. The only thing he still couldn't figure out was an old man with skin like leather, wrinkled and browned by the sun, that talked to him during the dream.

Was this just a dream? Ryan thought. No, maybe it was a vision.

Everything Ryan talked about and presented was something he felt like he had experienced. It had to be a vision!

His efforts paid off. Ryan received an A+ for the outstanding report and presentation of the Seasons Away. His teacher was curious as to how he learned some of the native language.

"It just came out. It felt natural to speak it," was his only reply. His classmates wanted to know more. They patted him on the back as he answered all their questions.

Ryan rushed home to spout the news of the report to his mother. She was waiting for him as he burst through the front door with the same excitement that he had when coming down the steps on Christmas morning. She was sitting on the edge of their recliner with her hands cupped over her chin, holding her head. She was sad. She wanted Ryan to walk with her into the kitchen because she had some "bad news." Ryan's heart sank. The excitement and joy he had carried home with him that day vanished as he walked into the kitchen with his mother.

# 7

Ryan stepped in the kitchen.

"Surprise!" screamed his mother, sister and father. His father had been out of town for six days selling automotive parts, brake pads, rotors and brake lines. He wasn't expected back home for another week. He had sold more than double his quota for the month to a large retail store that just opened in Farnsworth and was given a two-week vacation as a reward for selling so much merchandise.

Amazed and excited, Ryan was speechless. He was amazed that his mother was such a good actress, and excited that his father was home. This was not the end of the good news for Ryan, however. He was informed that a last-minute vacation to Yellowstone National Park had been planned. His mother had contacted the school to make sure everything was in order for Ryan and his sister, Shelly, to miss five days. Because they were going to Yellowstone and making some stops along the way, the school saw fit to excuse the kids, giving them an educational trip allowance. School policy stated that if the students turned in a report on the places visited and knowledge gained, they would be granted an "excused absence."

Still, Ryan had not heard the best part of the surprise. His parents knew of a Native-American reservation along their route. It was a fully functioning reservation but also a tourist attraction. His father knew exactly where the locale was and quickly pointed it out on the map. There were dances to observe, tee-pees to see and food to taste and buy. The clothing was also a big attraction. Pictures could be taken in actual Indian outfits. Such items like vests, necklaces, bracelets and headdresses could be purchased on the reservation as well.

"When are we leaving?" Ryan asked eagerly.

"First thing in the morning." replied his father. "So, get packing!"

"Mom," Ryan said, unable to wipe the smile from his face. "You were right. Mrs. Maslar is the best teacher I've ever had!"

Ryan raced past his sister, almost knocking her to the floor. He ran into to his room and began to pack.

"Ryan's Sixth-Grade graduation project was on the Pauwan," his mother told his father. "He was very proud of his work. Ryan got an A+ on the presentation. I was even told halfway through, he began to speak the language."

Ryan's father closed his eyes and smiled. "I think it's time to have a talk with my son," his father said.

"Yes, I believe it is," agreed his mother. Ryan's father made his way quietly up the stairs.

Standing in the doorway, his father asked, "Do you have everything packed?" Ryan nodded and continued stuffing his duffle bag.

"Ryan, sit here beside me." There was a silence that made Ryan uncomfortable. "You never met your grandfather. He was a very wise man. In fact, he was the wisest of his people."

"His people?" Ryan questioned.

Ryan's head tilted in confusion.

His father continued. "I was just a young man when I decided to leave. When I left, I lost contact with the members of my family. I never spoke to my father again. He was a proud man and could not understand why I wanted to leave the reservation and live as a white man. We were very different, your grandfather and I. Your grandfather wanted to hold on to the ways and traditions of the tribe."

Ryan nodded. "I wanted more," his father continued. "I wanted to travel, study and gain knowledge, experience technological advances." He paused. "I respect the traditions, but I always felt as though I was missing things in life." He patted Ryan's knee. "It was a very hard decision for me to make as a young man, but I knew if I was going to do anything, I had to leave the reservation."

Ryan's father finished. He smiled at his son. "You have the look of your grandfather. I've thought that since the day you were born. There is greatness in you. I can see it. One day you will have to recognize it for yourself." With a pat on the leg, his father stood and walked out of the room. Ryan had no questions for his father. He began to think about the language he spoke and how he must have come to know it. Things started to make a little sense.

He had everything he needed, including the book from the library he had taken out, placed on top of his clothes in his bag for easy access. From Philadelphia, the reservation was at least a sixteen-hour trip. What better way to pass the time than to read more about the lives of the Pauwan, the Native American people who as it turns out were his ancestors.

During the long drive, Ryan was able to finish the entire book. He now had more knowledge about his people than he had ever thought he would. He knew how the tribe supported itself; how every member had an important job to do to keep the tribe fed, clothed and safe. Even the children had a role, to watch carefully the jobs of the adults and learn what it is to be a productive member. No matter what the tribe was currently doing, the children were encouraged and expected to participate with the adults. This was a kind of "on the job training" and prepared the children for their future life.

The tribe was always successful in its hunts on the prairie. All members of the hunting party worked together in a controlled chaos to bring down many animals. Ryan had an enormous amount of respect for their entire way of life. His eyes became heavy as he placed the book on his lap. Ryan rested his chin in his hands and leaned his head against the car window. Heavy lids would not stay open and he quickly dozed off.

Finally, the family crossed the state line into South Dakota when the car hit a bump that awakened him. From here the reservation was only an hour away. He stared out the window of his father's company car, a wood-sided station wagon that was embarrassing for Ryan and his sister to be seen in.

Gazing across the endless prairie, Ryan saw a small gathering of teepees. Outside he saw women and children working on the hides of what appeared to be buffalo. Ryan closed his eyes and shook his head back and forth. When he opened his eyes and looked back, they were gone. They had vanished into the tall grass.

Ryan thought he was losing his mind, seeing things. He reached into the family cooler, grabbed a cold bottle of water and slugged it down. He thought maybe he was becoming dehydrated after the long trip. He used the bottle to wipe his forehead and glanced again out the window.

The people were back!

Ryan quickly pressed his nose against the glass. He couldn't believe what he was seeing. Just like that, the images faded once again into tall grass. Knowing he and his family were still an hour away, Ryan thought he would try to continue his nap before their arrival at the reservation. The images must have only appeared because he was jolted out of a deep sleep and exhausted from the long trip. Ryan put his head on a pillow and dozed off.

He began to dream about being a Lakota boy who was learning how to make and shoot a bow and arrow. He was also learning how to track and hunt. It was amazing!

The next thing Ryan knew, his father was shaking his arm, waking him to let him know they had arrived at a gas station that was located three miles from the reservation.

After drinking the entire bottle of water, Ryan needed to use the restroom. He walked into the store and was told that the restroom was around the back of the station. The attendant handed Ryan the key and pointed in the direction of the restroom. With his family still inside the store purchasing gas and a few snacks, Ryan rounded the corner and ran smack dab into something hard. Ryan staggered backwards and looked up to see what he had run into. He saw an old wrinkled man wearing only a pair of tattered pants, sitting on a stool just outside the restroom door. The man had no shirt or shoes on. He smiled at Ryan. His face was dark and wrinkled. His hair was long and gray. Ryan recognized him! It was the man from his dream.

The man began to speak. At first Ryan was afraid. He couldn't understand the words the old man was saying. He wasn't speaking English. Ryan wanted to run, but he couldn't. Try as he might, his feet wouldn't move. He was paralyzed. He just kept staring at the man as he spoke. Finally, the man said a few words Ryan knew.

"Look into your heart, your mind will become clear."

Ryan looked around as if to ask if the man was speaking to him.

"Yes, look deep inside and you will see clearly the path you are to take," said the man.

"Do I know you?" Ryan asked.

The old man smiled. "You have known me all your life, Little Hawk. You are only now beginning to recognize me."

Ryan was now terrified. He stumbled and fell backwards. He crawled on his hands and knees as he rounded the corner and got back on his feet, heading back to the car. He quickly climbed inside and sat quietly. Sweat streamed down his face. He saw his father round the corner, heading for the bathroom. Ryan realized that he still gripped the key tightly in his hand. His father quickly came back to the car and tapped on the window.

"Do you still have the key for the restroom, Ryan?" his father asked.

"What did you think of that crazy old man around the corner?" asked Ryan.

"What man?" his father replied, very puzzled by Ryan's question.

"You didn't see the old wrinkled man sitting on the stool by the bathroom?" Ryan's voice was shaking.

"No. What are you talking about, Ryan?" His father was now concerned.

Very concerned, Ryan's father quickly walked around the corner toward the restroom. Again, he saw nothing. He opened the door to the restroom and looked inside. Nobody was in or around the bathroom. He put his hands on his hips in confusion and returned to the car.

"There's nobody behind the building, Ryan. You must have imagined it. I looked around the corner and inside the restroom. I'm sorry, pal, I didn't see anyone."

Ryan jumped out of the car and sprinted behind the building. He saw nothing. No stool, no little wrinkled man, nothing! Just then, he was startled as a large owl flew from the ground and landed on the roof of the station, staring at him. Ryan didn't know what to think about the owl as he was completely bewildered by the events that had just unfolded.

He slowly walked back to the car, confused about what he had seen, or if he had seen it at all. He slinked into the back seat and slouched in embarrassment. Before his mother and sister returned to the car, Ryan realized that he had never used the restroom. Slowly he opened his car door and made his way to the bathroom. The owl was back. It stared annoyingly at Ryan until he stepped in its direction and shouted at it. The owl circled the station once, then flew out of sight. The bathroom door opened and his father stepped out, holding the door for his son to enter. Ryan walked in to relieve himself. When he was done, he stepped to the sink and washed his hands.

He looked into the foggy mirror and nearly fainted. The old wrinkled man was standing directly behind him.

Ryan turned as quickly as he could, but there was no one there. He began to sweat. Ryan wiped his forehead with a paper towel and headed quickly for the car. Sitting behind the wheel, his father saw the look of panic on Ryan's face. "You okay, son?" he asked.

"I'm not sure..." Ryan replied. "I think I see something, or someone, but I turn and they're gone!" he continued.

"You talking about 'the man' you saw?" asked his father. "I wouldn't be concerned about that," he added confidently, looking at Ryan through the rearview mirror. But Ryan wasn't so confident. So many things had taken place since the family crossed into Iowa. He was very unsure about continuing on with the trip.

# 8

The confusion from the gas station left Ryan feeling less excited about visiting the reservation. That is until he saw it appear along the horizon. Ryan suddenly became charged with energy. The reservation was so much different than he had ever imagined.

Entering the reservation reminded Ryan of entering a theme park. There was a large gate to pass through. Each car was first charged a fee to enter and then an additional fee to park. This was disappointing to Ryan. He never imagined the locale to be a for-profit organization.

Late spring was a busy time. Many tourists flocked to the reservation during this time of year. Several flowers and trees were in full blossom. The grass was a dark, rich green and felt like pillows under Ryan's feet. He slipped off his sandals and felt the soft grass tickle his toes. The sky was clear, not a cloud in sight. Now, far away from the large gate and parking lot, the colors of the teepees, grass and sky reminded Ryan of the beautiful reservation he had always imagined.

His family could request a tour guide to take them through the reservation. Ryan would not hear of this.

"I bet I know more about this place than any tour guide!" he remarked.

He thought that a tour guide would cheapen his experience. He wanted to see, hear and feel the surroundings of these people and how they once lived. He wanted to feel these things firsthand.

As Ryan's family made its way through the reservation and watched the many performances, Ryan noticed that he had become separated from them. He looked around, curiously at first. Then he thought, I'm by myself. Now they won't slow me down.

Ryan's father had given him $50.00 for doing such an outstanding job on his Sixth-Grade graduation project. His logic was to spend every cent. That way if he had no money left to bring home, he had no money for Jake to steal. He used the money to purchase several different items.

The first item was a necklace. Ryan was drawn to it upon first glance. The necklace called to him. It was made of claws; grizzly bear claws! The man at the table told the story of a young boy during his trial away from the tribe. The boy was full of courage and bravery. He had killed the bear and saved the lives of other boys from his tribe. The young boy made the necklace from the claws of the grizzly.

Ryan was fascinated by the story, thinking, What a brave boy to have killed such a terrifying beast. He had to have that necklace. He bought it and put it around his neck.

Immediately he saw a picture in his mind of a large bear charging toward him, bleeding badly from the neck. Ryan began to sweat. He could see an enormous paw with claws like swords, raised high in the air ready to end his life. Just then, the man who sold the necklace touched Ryan's shoulder.

"Are you alright?" the man asked. The touch and the man's question snapped him out of the daydream. Ryan's eyes were wide and his breathing short and fast as he answered the man and quickly walked to a different stand.

Hearing the shutter of a camera and seeing the puff of smoke from a flash, Ryan pushed opened a cracked door and walked into a small room. Here people could choose an outfit to wear and have a picture taken. The film used was old and it appeared as if the picture was taken a long time ago. Ryan chose an outfit and began to change. He looked at himself in the mirror wearing nothing more than a small headdress with two feathers, a loincloth and a pair of leggings made from the hide of a deer. Fringe dangled from the outside seams.

Another vision flashed in his mind. He was on the

trail of a great beast, following the tracks of a bear through the woods. Quickly it was gone. He took off the clothes after having the picture taken. He rubbed the photo in his hand and then put it in a small cardboard case for safekeeping before slipping it in his back pocket. Ryan moved on, becoming more confused about the flashbacks he was having.

At every stand, the items all seemingly had a story behind them. Ryan had also purchased a small pouch to hold artifacts that he could buy at other stands. The pouch was no exception. A boy and his father were on a hunt together. They had killed a large male buffalo. His father used part of the hide to make the pouch for his son. It would help them to remember their first hunt together. An actual arrowhead made hundreds of years ago, decorative feathers and beads were later purchased and placed in the pouch.

Ryan floated on air as he walked past an exhibit where a woman treated a buffalo hide. He heard the beating of a drum. He followed the sounds of the drum around a small food stand. Men performed a dance. Ryan sat down on the edge of the circle to watch.

He quickly realized this was a dance performed just before a hunt on the prairie. Several of the young men would gather around a fire and perform the dance to the spirits. This would entice the spirits of their ancestors to help them harvest the mighty buffalo.

Ryan sat quietly and watched as the dancers' feet stepped in perfect rhythm with the beating drums. He closed his eyes and the crowd of people disappeared. The sky turned from a pale blue to an almost black, as the sun had already set on the horizon. The brightness of the fire now lit the entire village.

The men danced fluently. One of them looked familiar. As the man came closer, Ryan thought the person looked just like his father's brother. Although he had never seen him in person, this man dancing resembled the man in pictures Ryan had seen. He invited Ryan to join in the dance. Ryan was very hesitant. Then he heard a voice from over his shoulder.

"Join them, Little Hawk," the voice said. Ryan turned to see who was talking to him. An old wrinkled man was sitting directly behind him. Not just any man...it was him, the man from the gas station.

Ryan immediately opened his eyes and jumped to his feet. The drums stopped. His heart beat rapidly and sweat dripped from his forehead. His chest heaved, desperately trying to take in as much air as he could. Ryan looked behind him, but there was no one there.

As he got up and looked around the circle, everyone was staring at him. One of the dancers even winked and nodded at Ryan.

"Did you hear that?" Ryan asked the woman sitting next to him.

"Hear what?" the woman asked.

"The man's voice. It said to join them," Ryan said frantically.

The woman looked at Ryan very strangely and asked, "Are you okay? Do you need something to drink?"

"No thank you," he said quietly.

Ryan didn't know what to make of the images he had seen. He began to think he was really losing his mind. He started to panic as he searched for his family. He ran from stand to stand. Ryan looked throughout the entire reservation and found nothing. He became frightened. He feared his family might have left him behind. He didn't know what to do.

Ryan became exhausted. Fatigue set in. He could hardly stand on his feet. Tears began to well in his eyes. Ryan frantically looked from right to left and then right again. The tears began to roll down his cheeks. Ryan knew he needed to rest and regain his wits. He looked just past the food court and spotted a small park bench. Quickly he made his way to it and sat.

Slowly he began to calm himself. A family sat staring at him. Their stares made Ryan uncomfortable. "Mommy, where are that boy's parents?" he heard the young girl ask. Ryan broke his eye contact with the mother. He got up and moved away from the bench before he could be approached. As Ryan made his way from the bench, a large bird swooped closely by, grabbing his attention. At first, he saw only a shadow cast as it silently glided by and landed in a small tree. It was an owl, the owl he had seen at the station. The bird focused all its attention on Ryan. It hopped in the air and with a few flaps of its powerful wings was airborne again. The owl flew a short distance and landed. It looked back at Ryan. He did not understand how or why, but he felt this bird's stares. He took a few steps in its direction and it flew again.

The scenario continued and Ryan was sure he was to keep following the bird. When the owl came to rest for the final time, it was perched atop an old teepee that was roped off, presented as an exhibit. Ryan's legs could carry him no further. He sat on the bare ground in exhaustion and closed his eyes. Ryan saw himself inside the teepee, barely clothed. He could hear drums beating loudly. He felt the soft fur floor under his feet. Ryan opened his eyes, believing that the owl had led him to the teepee for a reason. If he could rest a while inside the teepee, he would be reenergized to search once more for his family. He ducked underneath the rope and slipped past a guard into the nearby teepee.

The structure was an actual teepee that had been made and used by the plains Indians. A buffalo hide was used as the floor. Ryan also noticed wood and blankets. He slipped off his sandals and walked across the hide in his bare feet. He couldn't believe how soft the buffalo hide was. He paused and thought, Why would there be wood for a fire and blankets for sleeping if no one was ever in this thing?

He didn't bother wasting any more time with questions he couldn't answer. He grabbed the blanket, made from the hide of an antelope, and decided to lie down for a quick nap. Once he was rested, he would resume the search for his family. Ryan could hear the faint beating of drums. Oddly, the drums had a calmed him as the flap of the teepee had closed. Humming a song to the beat of the drums, he lay down and quickly fell asleep.

At first, he began to toss and turn. The thought of Jake ran through Ryan's mind. He dreamt that Jake found out he had spent the entire $50.00 on the reservation and didn't have any to fork over. "What would he do to me?" Ryan repeated in his dream.

The dream quickly shifted. Ryan dreamt that he was the boy who killed the bear. He tracked the awesome beast for two days, knowing it was stalking a boy from his own tribe.

The quick setting of an arrow and the precise placement into the beast's heart made the bear whirl around and charge at Ryan. But before it could do any harm, the fierce beast had stumbled and fallen at his feet.

Ryan saw the enormous claws and thought he would make a necklace to always remember the day he killed the bear and saved an Indian brother.

Ryan began to wake from his nap. He heard the drums still beating just as they were when he had fallen asleep. He awoke refreshed and ready to start searching for his family again.

# 9

Voices were heard outside the teepee. At first Ryan could not understand what they were saying. It was some sort of foreign language. As he emerged from the teepee and rubbed the sleep from his eyes, Ryan looked around the reservation. He spoke to an old woman dressed completely in Indian clothing. He used words he had never spoken before, but he was comfortable using the language. Something else was different. He felt a gentle breeze across his legs. He became alarmed.

He suddenly stopped, dropped the pouch he was holding and ran back inside the teepee. He was shocked to see a fire burning. The smoke rose and escaped through a hole at the top of the structure.

"What is going on?" he asked himself. "Where am I? What is going on?"

He sprinted back outside and down toward the parking lot. There was nothing. No parking lot, no gate...only a vast sea of green grass swaying in the fresh spring air.

Ryan was shocked. He examined his clothing. He was nearly naked. Only a loincloth covered his waist and he wore nothing over his legs, back or shoulders. He sat on the ground and began to sob. His father, mother and sister were gone. What was he to do? The people around him were strangers. "How did I get here?" he asked himself.

Ryan then heard a voice speak to him.

"Are you ready for today's lesson, Little Hawk?" the voice asked softly in a language he knew, but wasn't English. Ryan turned to face whomever was speaking to him. An older woman with long black hair, braided tightly to her head, stood over him. She looked much like his mother. Could it be?

"Mom?" Ryan asked. "Is that you?"

"Of course it is, Son. Who did you think it would be?" she answered.

"How did we get here?" he asked.

"Are you feeling alright, Little Hawk?" his mother asked. "You didn't sleep well. You were tossing and turning all night. You were even saying some strange things, speaking in a different tongue."

He was very confused. Ryan looked around only to see a young woman cleaning the underside of a buffalo hide. She glanced up and smiled at Ryan. This girl looked just like his sister, Shelly. She put her head back down and focused on the task at hand.

Ryan spent the morning with his mother, Netis, learning how to preserve meat. He watched her closely.

First Netis had taken the hindquarters of an antelope and cut them into chunks. Then she sliced the chunks into thin slivers, placing them high over the fire. She explained to Ryan that this process would very slowly cook and dry the meat so that it could be stored for eating later. The smoke would help to cook the meat and add taste. The entire process would take a day's time. Ryan thought that the meat was just like the beef jerky he had in his snack at school. And it was.

For the entire morning, Ryan was so involved with his mother and working with the meat he had completely forgotten about his present situation. Netis turned and asked if he was going to put this into his journal. His family thought the journal was unnecessary. Their people had no written language. Traditions and stories were passed from generation to generation orally. Ryan was the first to put information into a journal.

He watched as his mother walked swiftly around the teepee and went inside. The flap opened and Netis stepped out. "Here," she said. "You forgot it this morning." And she handed him the journal. He began to draw pictures, rough sketches of the important facts about preserving meat. He looked at the feather in his hand and dipped it into the small bowl containing blackberry juice. It was then that he realized he was truly in a different time.

The following morning was used to instruct Little Hawk on how to take the hides of animals and properly clean them of all fat and hair. He was sent to gather ashes from a fire that had burned down the night before. Netis was digging a shallow hole in the ground and lining it with clay. Upon his arrival, he was told to dump the ashes in the hole and slowly mix them with water. When the soupy mixture was ready, an antelope hide was dropped in. Netis made sure it was completely submerged, to be left there for a day's time. Little Hawk was told that urine could be sometimes added to help speed up the process. This concoction would help to break down the hide and speed up the process of removing the hair.

Little Hawk found out firsthand that this was the easy part. Netis took a hide that had already soaked in the solution for a day and draped it over the side of a log. She handed Little Hawk a flat shoulder bone and instructed him on the proper angle at which to take the hair off most efficiently. She let him attempt this on his own. Again, she told him of the angle. Still he didn't have much success. Netis could sense Little Hawk's frustration, so she gently placed her hand over his and began to remove the hair easily. He nodded in approval and gratitude, then continued to remove all the hair. Again, it was set to dry. The work was grueling and difficult, but something that he had to master to survive.

Next Netis and her son went to a large buffalo hide that had been cleaned of all bodily material and was staked out to dry. Little Hawk was told to feel the hide before they started to work on it. "It is hard and rough to the touch," Little Hawk told Netis. That's when she told him he needed to use the brain.

Brain power was used on the articles that were to be worn or used as blankets. If a piece of hide was just treated and cleaned of all hair, blood or fat, it would become very hard and stiff. Little Hawk's mother showed him just how to prevent such a thing from happening.

"You must use your brain," Netis told him.

"How?" he asked.

"You know that we use as much of a downed animal as we possibly can," she nodded, then continued, "We will use the brain." Netis took the brain of a buffalo and placed it into a bowl of water. Gently, they both started kneading the brain until it began to dissolve in the water. When it became a fine slurry, the mixture was softly massaged into the skin side of a hide. After every inch of the underside was coated, mother and son folded it only once to ensure that the brainy solution would not contact the hairy side of the hide. "We will wait until tomorrow. Then we will open it to dry."

Little Hawk watched his mother place six poles around a fire and connect them with thin rope material at the top. Netis started to wrap the hide around the poles at the bottom and finished at the top to form a cone-like shape. The creation reminded Little Hawk of a small teepee. The smoke from the fire would permeate the hide and change its color. When the hide turned a golden brown, it was ready to be used or worn.

"The hide will be soft and pliable to be draped over your shoulders or used as a blanket. Know that if it would get wet, it will become hard when it dries. If this happens, you must repeat this process to keep the hide soft."

Hides of animals had many different uses. Some were used as clothing, others as blankets. Knowing what each hide would eventually become dictated if the hair was removed or preserved. Learning how to treat a hide was essential for Little Hawk to master.

Little Hawk left his mother and sat to look in his journal. He observed what he had already drawn. He started to remember actually drawing what appeared on the pages. Everything was now becoming so familiar to Ryan. He knew members of the tribe by name. He knew what they did and their importance to the tribe. He became more comfortable with and used to answering to his name, Little Hawk.

The time with his mother passed quickly and soon

Little Hawk joined his father and uncle. They sat to talk at the midday meal. The three shared cornbread next to a fire. The two older men began to discuss a dream/vision that one of them had. Light as a Feather was Little Hawk's uncle and the brother of Rolling Thunder. The vision he had was of people dressed in funny clothes. These men came in great numbers across their land. Some were friendly. Others were not. Rolling Thunder, the father of Little Hawk, was greatly concerned about this vision. They decided the two would sit with the chief and inform him of the vision. Neither of them, nor Little Hawk, would speak of this again until they had a chance to speak to Chief Strong Bow. They would not want fear to spread throughout the village.

The conversation shifted to the fast approaching Seasons Away. Stories were told and laughs were had about the two men and their experiences. Rolling Thunder told of a time when he was caught in his own snare. At first, he didn't realize that he was held fast by his own contraption. He tugged and pulled his leg, trying to get himself free. With each pull, every tug, the snare got tighter and tighter around his ankle. Finally, Rolling Thunder looked down and chuckled to himself as he realized he was caught in one of his own devices. "At least I knew I made a good snare," he said as the three laughed.

The conversation helped to calm the nerves of

Little Hawk. It was funny for him to think of his father making such a silly mistake, forgetting where he put his traps. Next to Chief Strong Bow, Rolling Thunder was the wisest man in the tribe. Everyone looked to him before taking any thoughts or concerns before the chief. He was tall and broad across the shoulders. His waist was slim and rippled like that of a shallow moving stream. He stood proudly when speaking to his tribe or when speaking to any member of a neighboring tribe. When Little Hawk was younger, he poked his father one morning to wake him. He remembered it was like poking a boulder of solid granite. All members of the tribe respected Rolling Thunder. Even though he felt a tremendous amount of pressure, Little Hawk was proud to be his son.

After the midday meal, Little Hawk had accompanied Light as a Feather into the area just outside the village. There were small groups of trees growing toward the east. Small groves of aspen and ash trees were most common.

Little Hawk knew exactly how his uncle had received his name. He was an excellent hunter and tracker. He walked in such a manner that even the deer couldn't hear him coming. He walked as though he was as light as a feather.

Little Hawk took his journal everywhere he went because he wanted to remember everything exactly how it was told to him. Little Hawk was the only person in his family to use a journal. In fact, there was no written language among the tribe. Little Hawk's family thought it was strange that he carried it with him so often. Because it helped him feel more confident about everything he was learning, they saw no harm in it and let it be. He would spend much of the time sketching the main points of each lesson, drawing small pictures to help him remember.

One lesson Light as a Feather taught him was to walk quietly.

"The eyes are most important," whispered his uncle, "you must scan the entire area."

"For game?" asked Little Hawk.

"Not only for game," answered Light as a Feather, "but also for objects on the trail you are walking."

"The forest floor can be as loud or as quiet as you want it to be," explained his uncle. "Looking out for litter on the trail is very important. You don't want to step on any twigs or loose leaves and make a noise."

Light as a Feather and his young nephew went to a well-run deer trail. These were the first tracks Little Hawk drew in his journal. They were long and thin. One end of the track was thinner and came to a point. At the other end, separated from the long, thin section, was a dot.

Light as a Feather told him, "The tracks are those of

a deer, Little Hawk. It was here this morning. The deer walked from the stream and across the hillside."

"How do you know all that just from looking at these tracks?"

"The tracks are easily recognized," said Light as a Feather. "The thinner end of the track, or point, helps to let us know the direction it was heading. The two dots also help. They appear behind the track. It rained last night, yes?"

"Yes, it did," answered Little Hawk.

"The rain washed the old tracks away. It stopped early this morning," his uncle explained. "After the rain stopped, the deer walked this path, leaving its tracks behind. The sun is moving through the sky into the late afternoon. The deer passed through here between the time it had stopped raining, and now."

Little Hawk looked at the tracks in amazement. All that information was right in front of him, yet he failed to gather it until now.

Light as a Feather then took Little Hawk to a creek bottom. He asked Little Hawk if he recognized the tracks that had appeared on the creek bank. Little Hawk knew immediately these were the tracks of a bear.

"Not only a bear, but a grizzly bear," remarked his uncle.

"How are you able to tell the difference between a black bear and a grizzly bear, just by looking at the tracks?" asked Little Hawk.

"Look closely at the smaller tracks. These are the front paws. They are slightly turned in, pointing to each other. These are the tracks of a grizzly. Black bear paws point straight ahead, in the direction the bear is walking," explained Light as a Feather. "This is a small grizzly, only two years of age. It was just separated from its mother. The paws are not much bigger than the width of my hand."

"How big are the tracks of a full grown male grizzly?" Little Hawk asked.

"You'll know when you see them. They are larger than both of your hands put together," said Light as a Feather. Little Hawk lifted his hands, put them together and stared at them.

"Know this Little Hawk," his uncle said seriously, "the grizzly is a ferocious beast. Once it tastes human blood, human blood is all it will want. The grizzly is cunning and smart. It will follow at a long distance keeping you in sight and also in smell. It will pattern you, knowing where and when you will be in a certain place. You must always be aware of the tracks it will leave."

"It will hunt us?" Little Hawk asked in amazement.

"Yes," said his uncle. "You must always be aware of your surroundings."

Little Hawk sat quietly, drawing the shape of the deer and bear tracks. He also made a note of the grizzly bear's front paws pointing toward each other.

This lesson took most of the afternoon. Little Hawk and Light as a Feather then returned to the tribe. Little Hawk's father was waiting for him. They sat to talk and eat before the third lesson of the day.

Little Hawk said very little during the meal. He spent most of the time looking at the pictures of other lessons his uncle had taught him. He recognized the entry about trapping. He remembered how his uncle taught him to find the roots of small trees, strip them of their bark and make them into a thin rope to make a snare trap for smaller prey, such as a rabbit or a grouse. The memories of all those lessons came roaring back. Little Hawk then began to remember the lessons his father was teaching him.

Rolling Thunder was teaching him how to make a bow, arrows and arrowheads. All male adults in the tribe received their names based on something about their personality or an event that helped to shape them into the person they became. Little Hawk's father was no exception. He received his name based on the volume and strength of his voice. When he spoke, his loud, deep voice demanded that people listen. It echoed through the village and seemed to make the teepees shake. Everyone in the village would stop whatever it is they were doing and give Rolling Thunder their undivided attention when he spoke.

Little Hawk, again, opened his journal and began to look at previous lessons. He and his father had already chosen the ash tree to make a bow. The sapling was three inches in diameter and four feet in length.

The second step was to de-bark and carve the sapling. This was done by widdling the chosen piece with a knife. Once that was finished, a rough stone was then used to smooth the exposed wood.

The next two steps were to shape the sapling. First, it would be tapered from the thickest part, being the middle, to each end of wood. The ends were much slimmer than the middle to help create flexibility in the bow. Then the ends would be drawn toward each other ever so slightly. This was accomplished by placing different sized strings on the bow. The strings used to shape the wood were made from long pieces of grass woven tightly together. Standing as one, a blade of grass was very weak. When several pieces were woven tightly together, however, the material became very strong and couldn't be pulled apart. Each day, the string would be changed and a smaller string added. This would apply pressure to the wood and hold it there for a day's time. Every few hours, water had to be applied to the bow. If this didn't happen, the wood would become dry and splinter. Beeswax would also be rubbed along the shaft of the bow. This, too, would help prevent splintering.

Continued over a week's time, water and pressure

added to the wood would transform what was once a sapling into an accurate shooting weapon.

The finishing touches to any bow are left to the person making it. The handle and unique carvings would distinguish one bow from another, as different as the person making the bow.

Little Hawk's bow was a masterpiece. It was darker than any other bow his father had ever seen. The colors flowed through it like the river through tall grass. The handle on this bow was more slender because Little Hawk had unusually small hands. Rolling Thunder helped Little Hawk carve several small pictures into the limbs of the bow. One picture was of an eagle soaring high in the sky. The other was of the sun. Little Hawk chose these because the eagle was a bird of prey and a symbol of strength and honor. The sun was also a symbol of strength as the giver of life to the earth.

The bow and string were made at the same time. The string for shooting the bow was made from a material called a sinew. This came from an animal, usually a tendon of a buffalo. A sinew was very strong and elastic. The tendon from the hind leg of a buffalo could be taken and soaked in water. Each day the tendon was stretched and then set out to dry. The process was repeated until the sinew was long enough to be placed tightly on each end of the bow. When finished, the bow was a work of art. Beeswax was also rubbed over the string to keep it from drying out and snapping.

The next lesson involved taking the limbs of an ash tree to make the arrows. The bark was stripped and the wood was rubbed smooth. The arrowhead would be slid into a notch and held firm to the shaft using a thin piece of sinew. It was a tedious task, one that would take a skillful hand to master. Little Hawk had to take it seriously if his arrows were to fly true.

The final touch on an arrow would be the placement of the feathers. Normally, three feathers would be placed at the rear of the shaft, helping the arrow to fly straight. Little Hawk and Rolling Thunder had made several arrows, enough to fill Little Hawk's quiver with a dozen.

With Little Hawk's day almost over and final lesson here, he strolled casually through the village, looking at every lesson in the journal. The sun was setting on the horizon as Little Hawk entered the teepee of his grandfather, Kicking Bird.

He walked in and sat on the north end of the teepee, close to the fire. The flap opened and Kicking Bird stepped inside. His head was down so that Little Hawk could not see his face. His hair was long and gray. He had no shirt on, exposing his dark and wrinkled skin.

Kicking Bird walked closer to the fire, shedding light on his face.

"It's you!" shouted Little Hawk.

"Yes, it is me, Kicking Bird...your grandfather," the old man said. "I am brother to Chief Strong Bow."

"You were at the gas station and on the reservation! You told me to dance with the men!" shouted Little Hawk.

"I have told you many things, Little Hawk," his grandfather replied. He smiled, looking very pleased that Little Hawk had recognized him. "Are you ready to begin today?"

"Yes, I am ready," a confused Little Hawk answered.

His grandfather began to tell him about the bond between man and spirit. He explained to Little Hawk the importance of the past, and how knowing where one has been can help to shed light on the direction one is going.

"Through our visions, we can see the direction we are to go," Kicking Bird said. "But when you are truly lost and have no direction, then you must look to the spirits for guidance."

He taught his grandson how to look into the world of the spirits. Little Hawk was confused but didn't let his grandfather see his confusion. He wrote everything in his journal. A special plant was used as the main ingredient. He drew pictures of the plant. To look into the spirit world, it must be heated and mixed with water. Once prepared, it was swallowed.

"Remember, Little Hawk, when you have come to a

point where you are lost and have no direction, look to our ancestors," Kicking Bird told him. "They will show you the way."

"Grandfather, I have had a dream. I have had it almost every night since I can remember," explained Little Hawk.

He continued to tell his grandfather about the bear that had haunted his dreams for years. He told him of the saliva that dripped from its tongue and teeth as it was ready to end his life. Kicking Bird explained to Little Hawk that his dream was trying to give him a look at something he will face in the future. "The bear may have something to do with a boy that you are having trouble with?" his grandfather added.

Little Hawk didn't reply. His grandfather was trying to get him to open up and talk about the trouble he had with Running Bear but he did no such thing.

His grandfather nodded, acknowledging that Little Hawk didn't want to speak about his own troubles. "I have seen that one day you will have to make a decision regarding this boy," Kicking Bird said slowly. Still, Little Hawk said nothing. He stared at the fire, remembering all the things that Running Bear had done. From the time he could first remember as a younger child, Running Bear was rotten. "A bad seed," Little Hawk's mother called him. She would often ask, "How could so much anger and hatred be in such a small child?"

Others in the tribe tried to understand why Running Bear was this way. When he was very young, Running Bear had seen his father brutally attacked and killed by another tribe. His mother, Ptaysanwee, did the best she could, but was always met with hostility from her son. His mother was in a constant state of sadness, having never recovered from the loss of her husband and then enduring the sorrow of watching her son treat others in a manner that was not in the keepings of the tribe. Heaviness settled in her chest and would not leave. Many times, she asked for help from the other women in the village. It was no use. He pushed them all away.

Normally the boys and girls of the tribe had very few confrontations. Arguing and fighting among the children were almost nonexistent. That is except for Running Bear. He had trouble with almost everyone, including Little Hawk. The only people he would even speak to were two other boys, Muskrat and Tiny Beaver. They would do anything Running Bear said. They would never question his command. They would carry out whatever he said to do.

The only time Little Hawk remembered a conflict was when all the men were preparing to confront a neighboring village because they had attacked and killed a member of their tribe. That member was Running Bear's dad. Little Hawk watched as the men smashed berries they found from the forest. Brilliant colors were made...reds, blues and whites. Every brave colored his body. Faces, chests and backs, and even parts of their legs, were covered in what they called war paint. Their horses were spotted with handprints of red and blue.

The men of Little Hawk's tribe confronted the smaller war party and things were made even. One warrior from the other tribe was killed and several others were injured in the skirmish. The chiefs then met. Rolling Thunder was at Chief Strong Bow's side and a deal was struck. Peace would once again rule the land.

Little Hawk thought of Running Bear and what might have happened if someone so cold and cruel was the person to negotiate such deals. It made him shiver at the very thought of wiping out an entire tribe.

Little Hawk's thoughts then shifted to the Seasons Away as he walked a few miles away from the tribe. He sat by the creek-side, looking at his journal and thinking about what his grandfather had told him.

He started to nod off and fall asleep when he heard a twig snap in the dense brush behind him. He quickly jumped to his feet, dropping his journal, but was alert. From the bushes came a blood-curdling scream, then out jumped Running Bear.

He looked exactly like Jake Farlow! Little Hawk's jaw almost hit the ground! It was him! He was sure of it!

How could this be? Little Hawk thought to himself. How did he get here? Little Hawk stumbled backward.

Running Bear quickly raced towards Little Hawk, startling him. He began to circle Little Hawk and then called to the others who were waiting in the brush.

Tiny Beaver and Muskrat were upon Little Hawk in the blink of an eye. It was Little Hawk's worst nightmare.

"But how?" he thought to himself.

They too circled. They began to poke at Little Hawk and push him to the ground. Every attempt to regain his footing was thwarted by one of the boys who kicked Little Hawk back to the ground. Then Running Bear ripped the necklace from around Little Hawk's neck and kept it for himself.

Little Hawk's sister crouched behind thick brush and watched in horror as Running Bear and the others had assaulted her younger brother. Aahana, which means "First Rays of Light," was so named because she was born at dawn. She wanted to spring from her hidden position and defend Little Hawk, but she stayed put. She knew that was not her place. Aahana realized this would only make things worse for him. Little Hawk would be shamed if a girl came to his defense and rescued him.

# 10

Aahana was strong, fast and independent. Her mother and father were very proud of her independence and strong spirit. On the verge of her thirteenth birthday, Aahana had begged and pleaded with her father to let her experience the Seasons Away. He would not hear of this. Women were to stay within the protection of the village as much as possible. Rolling Thunder tried to explain to his daughter that the rules and traditions of the tribe wouldn't permit such a thing to happen.

"I am strong, Father! Stronger than many of the boys my age!" Aahana's voice was loud, louder than she realized, a gift she had inherited from her father. Her tongue was sharp and Rolling Thunder was not pleased with such a tone.

"Do not speak to me in that tone Aahana!" Rolling Thunder said. "I see the strength and intelligence in you and have all the confidence that you would do well during the time away from the tribe. However, the tribe will not hear of such a thing. A girl, alone in the wilderness..." Rolling Thunder paused and then finished. "That is not going to happen."

Aahana stared at the ground, disappointed with the decision her father made.

"What we can do?" Rolling Thunder gently lifted his daughter's chin and held it in his huge, rough hand. He stared at his beautiful daughter, smiled and then said, "What we can do is train as if you will be confronting the elements of the wilderness. Only the two of us can know of this." Aahana smiled at her father. A small victory, Aahana thought, but a victory nonetheless.

They started with the very basics of defense. Rolling Thunder taught his daughter to defend her position. "What does that mean, Father?" Aahana asked. Rolling Thunder was very patient with his eager daughter.

"If you were to go after someone and attack them, your mind will be clouded with anger." he explained. "Continuing to lunge and swing wildly at an opponent will tire your arms and legs quickly. Then he will have the advantage, as you will be too tired to defend yourself."

Aahana listened intently to her father's advice. She never needed anything to be repeated, as her mind was a steel trap.

Rolling Thunder continued. "When your opponent attempts to strike, wait until the very last moment and then step to the side, avoiding the contact." In slow motion, he drew a fist and began to swing at his daughter. He told her the exact moment to move and step to her left. She did as she was told. As his strike went past Aahana's face, his momentum carried him well past her.

"At this point you can do as you wish," Rolling Thunder said earnestly. "Shove me to the ground or just step back and be ready to move again. Stay on your toes so that you can be like the lightning. Swift and fast."

The lesson then began to gain speed as Rolling Thunder asked Aahana to try her best to strike him on the chin. Aahana ran toward her father and swung wildly, trying to connect with a punch, but found herself sprawled across the ground, face down in the dirt. She became angry and jumped to her feet. She eyed her father, who was crouched, knees bent, arms up and fists clenched. But instead of lunging wildly again, she stopped and smiled at her father. He stood erect and smiled back. Aahana realized exactly what Rolling Thunder had meant by defending her position.

The lesson continued with Rolling Thunder walking through every step or action, later speeding things up so that Aahana could react quickly to various situations. He came at her from all angles...the front, side and rear. He taught her how to block punches with her forearms and shins.

The memories of these lessons played in her mind as Aahana watched the final blow land in Little Hawk's midsection. She could tell it took his breath away as he doubled over and gasped for air. Aahana closed her eyes and lowered her head, as she didn't want to watch any more of this.

As quickly as the boys were on Little Hawk, they were gone again. He picked up the journal and thought that dropping it was a good thing. Running Bear would have surely destroyed the book.

Little Hawk sat for a long time confused about what had just occurred. He slowly walked back to the tribe, trying to figure out what was going on. He then had to think of something to tell his mother, for she had made the necklace.

Little Hawk had no idea that his sister had witnessed the harassment. He was ashamed and felt as helpless as a newborn baby. "Will this ever end?" Little Hawk asked himself.

Aahana thought of a plan that would pass on the knowledge her father secretly gave to her. After Running Bear and the others had gone, Aahana watched as Little Hawk slowly walked toward the village. She stepped out onto the path he was walking on and confronted him.

"Why do you not defend yourself?" Aahana asked.

Little Hawk put his head down and tried to walk past his sister, ignoring the question. His sister was persistent and asked again. This time she put her hand on his chest, stopping him in his tracks.

"I don't know what you are talking about," Little Hawk answered.

"I watched what happened! I saw what Running Bear did!" Aahana raised her voice. Little Hawk snapped. "There are three of them! What am I supposed to do?"

"I can help you," Aahana said. But before she could continue, Little Hawk yelled, "That's just what I need, my sister fighting my battles for me! I would be the laughingstock of the entire village."

"What we can do..." Aahana began to say but was cut off again.

"We can't do anything," Little Hawk said. "I will always have to put up with Running Bear."

"Do you want to learn how to defend yourself?"

"Sure, but who would teach me? Everyone is already busy preparing me for the Seasons Away."

"I will train you," Aahana said.

"Don't be silly. You can't train me. You're a girl! How would you train me?"

"Father trained me," she whispered. "I will teach you everything he taught me." Aahana always had a way of convincing her brother. After a bit of hesitation, he accepted. And with that, Aahana was quite satisfied.

Little Hawk knew his sister wasn't like the other girls in the tribe. She was serious in every aspect of her life. When others laughed and played, Aahana was talking with her mother, gathering information that would help her in the future. If she did take time to play, she took the rules of the game seriously. Her demeanor took the fun out of the game for the other girls and they rarely asked her to play. Their mother, Netis, would often say she wished her daughter wouldn't take everything in life so seriously. Little Hawk, however, knew his sister's focus and seriousness would be exactly what he needed. It was decided when the two had any free time that they would meet just outside the village to train. They split and went their separate ways.

When Little Hawk got back to the tribe, his mother noticed right away the necklace was missing. Little Hawk manufactured a lie, telling her he was running through the woods and that it had caught on a twig. The necklace had fallen into a stream and he could not retrieve it.

Little Hawk's mother had wanted to know where exactly the accident happened. She said that she could search the stream for the necklace. Little Hawk then assured his mother that he had searched long and hard for the necklace to no avail. The necklace was gone.

He began to think about all the other items and possessions that were important to him. Then he thought about Running Bear and how he had taken most of them. He knew it was not the way of his people, to take and steal from one another. He became angry. Then Little Hawk remembered his parents always telling him to treat others as you would like to be treated, and those words quickly calmed him.

Within days of the confrontation with Running Bear where his necklace was taken, Little Hawk met his sister and they secretly made their way to the outskirts of the village. Aahana chose a spot very close to a burial ground. This place was chosen because no one from the tribe would venture close to that area. Little Hawk was apprehensive about being so close to the burial site but was assured by his sister that they were not disrespecting any of their ancestors.

First, Aahana had Little Hawk clench his hand into a fist and swing at her. He refused. She commanded Little Hawk to swing. He did so but did not swing hard. His sister yelled this time to swing hard, like he meant it. Again, he made a halfhearted attempt. This time she shoved Little Hawk and screamed at him to swing at her. Instantly, he became angry and swung with all his might, trying to land his fist on her chin. With cat-like reflexes, Aahana ducked the punch. She stepped to the side and grabbed Little Hawk by the wrist. She pulled him forward and tripped Little Hawk at the same time. In the blink of an eye, he was lying on the ground. He was flat on his back, trying to figure out what just happened.

Aahana extended her hand and helped her brother to his feet.

"How did you do that?" Little Hawk asked in amazement.

"I used your momentum against you," his sister replied. "All your force was coming toward me in one direction. I just stepped out of the way of your punch and gave you a shove. Your own momentum carried you to the ground." She continued, "We could do this all day. Soon you would tire and at that point I could strike at you without any resistance." There was a pause. "Or I could simply walk away and leave you gasping for air on the ground. That would be your decision to make."

It was all making sense now to Little Hawk. He remembered his father and sister disappearing from the tribe from time to time. Now he knew what they were up to. He also realized just how strong and clever his sister really was.

"You are quick and strong, Aahana," Little Hawk said. "I am proud you are my sister."

The two talked much of the afternoon as Little Hawk learned how to defend himself. Every step was shown to him in slow motion. The position of his hands and feet were critical. Every step was practiced over and over again until it was mastered. So, brother and sister met every spare moment they had. With every lesson, Little Hawk grew stronger and quicker and his sister's pride in her brother also grew. And something else happened. Little Hawk and Aahana grew closer than ever. In the past, Little Hawk was always a bit jealous of his sister. She did everything so well. Now jealousy was replaced with pride and admiration for Aahana.

Knowing he was preparing to leave the village soon, Little Hawk wanted to give some sort of gift to his sister, something that would show her how much he appreciated the time she spent with him and the valuable knowledge he gained from her. Little Hawk could think of no possession he had that would be worthy of Aahana.

"One day, I will present you with a gift that will match the admiration I have for you in my heart," Little Hawk said to his sister.

"No such gift is needed," was her only reply. She placed her hands on Little Hawk's shoulders. But before she could say another word, he surprised Aahana and threw his arms around her and squeezed as hard as he could. She embraced her younger brother and gently rested her chin on the top of his head and whispered. "You have great strength and courage inside you. One day, it will be proven to all of the village."

"Thank you for everything," Little Hawk said back.

With the day of departure rapidly approaching, Little Hawk's father walked with him to give some last words of encouragement.

"I see you and your sister have grown close," Rolling Thunder began. "Aahana is strong and intelligent," Little

Hawk replied. "I am proud to be her brother."

"I am a proud father as well," Rolling Thunder nodded his head as he spoke. He went on and told Little Hawk of his Seasons Away. He spoke of finding somewhere to stay that would keep him safe and dry. Rolling Thunder told Little Hawk how he had kept track of the days by scratching marks on the cave walls and drawing pictures to pass the time. He made a reference to Little Hawk's journal and how the pictures on the wall were like the ones in his journal.

Earlier, Little Hawk felt fear and anxiety about leaving his parents for such a long time. Now that he had spoken to his father, those feelings were gone. He looked at his journal and thought that if he used it to help him remember all he was taught, he couldn't go wrong.

# 11

The night of the ceremony, Little Hawk was excited. He was filled with confidence. With his journal in hand, he felt as though the Seasons Away would be an amazing experience. To this point in his life, Little Hawk had always tagged along on hunts and observed, sometimes participating in other preparations, but never had full responsibility for anything. Soon he would be completely on his own, relying only on himself to survive.

Everything was happening so quickly that Little Hawk had no time to thank his family for all they had done and taught him. There were only four boys of age for the Seasons Away. They were brought before the tribal council and the chief. The drums that had been beating loudly were now silent. The rattles made several generations ago were now quiet as well. Only the crackling of the fire could be heard, until the chief began to speak.

"We have gathered on this glorious evening to send our four young boys off to become men."

Little Hawk could hear the words of Chief Strong Bow but was more affected by the look on his father's face, a look of confidence and pride. He glanced over his father's shoulder to see the same look on the face of Light as a Feather. He focused once again on the words of the chief as he finished.

"Each of you knows the importance of this journey. You all know the rules and that they are not to be broken. You have been taught well. Take this information with you and use it to the best of your ability. Let the spirits of your forefathers guide you as you take the first steps of becoming a man. The tribe cannot and will not assist you in any way. You may not return to the tribe for any reason."

Just then Running Bear shoved Little Hawk forward. He stumbled and fell to his knees. The chief stopped talking. With all eyes fixed on Chief Strong Bow, no one saw what Running Bear had done. Little Hawk quickly jumped to his feet and reclaimed his position in line. He stared at Running Bear. Running Bear glared back. Little Hawk quickly looked to the ground, breaking any eye contact.

Chief Strong Bow continued. "You have been taught by us everything you will need to know. Other lessons, you will learn. The wilderness has much to teach you. At first light we will send you into the forest to build your sweat lodge and take your first steps to becoming a man. After one day's time, you will report to me and speak of the things you saw in the lodge. Good luck."

With the words of the chief echoing in his mind, Little Hawk could not sleep. He knew at first light he would say goodbye to his family and begin his journey. He tossed and turned most of the night. He finally fell asleep and began to dream about being away from the tribe. Everything was great until Running Bear attacked him. Running Bear was shaking him, calling his name.

"Little Hawk ... Little Hawk!"

When he opened his eyes, his father was standing over him.

"It is time my son. Your journey begins today," his father said.

Little Hawk and his father gathered what they needed and headed to the forest. They found a spot next to the stream and began to build a lodge.

The two worked hard to cut several young trees and strip them of their bark. They used the bark as rope to tie the bent over trees together. Several hides were used to cover the outside of the lodge. Finally, the fire pit was dug in the structure's center. The pit was lined with stones from the creek.

Little Hawk started a fire and began to fill the inside of the lodge with heat. When the fire got so hot that the rocks began to crack, Little Hawk poured water over them. An intense steam filled the lodge. Little Hawk repeated this action several times throughout the night.

He sat for the longest time waiting for something to happen. He actually became bored while sitting there and thought about leaving the lodge. But he knew how disappointed his father would be and stayed put.

Little Hawk knew he was not permitted to sleep even though the heat inside made him feel terribly exhausted. He became disoriented as he began to see an owl sitting on a branch high overhead. He reached into the air as if trying to touch the bird but couldn't. Little Hawk saw himself walking through the forest and thought he was dreaming. He seemed to be followed everywhere by this owl. When he stopped, it stopped. The owl watched him closely. He realized he was still inside the lodge and came to his wits. Little Hawk heard a voice coming from outside. Rolling Thunder was calling for him to return.

Little Hawk made his way back to the tribe. He talked to his grandfather and the chief. He told them of the owl and how it followed him everywhere. The two old men looked pleased with this vision. He was told that the owl would be the spirit that would follow him throughout his journey to become a man. The owl meant that Little Hawk would have great wisdom as he fought through a rough time during his Seasons Away. At first this troubled Little Hawk. He could only think about the forthcoming "rough times" and what exactly that meant.

Little Hawk joined Rolling Thunder continuing to be concerned about the vision. They walked steadily through the village and made their way into Rolling Thunder's quarters.

"Father, they told me that the owl I saw meant great wisdom. I would need that wisdom when facing a difficult situation. What do you think was meant by the rough times I will have during the Seasons Away?" Little Hawk asked.

Not wanting to frighten his son, Rolling Thunder was straightforward when he replied. "There will be times to make serious decisions during your Seasons Away. Remember, the owl means you will meet those decisions with wisdom." These words calmed Little Hawk as he looked his father in the eye. Slowly Little Hawk turned to walk away.

"Little Hawk, I have something for you," his father said.

He stopped to face his father. He glanced down to look at his possessions. They consisted of a knife (made from the antler of a deer with both sides ground to a razor-sharp edge), a small hatchet (made from the shoulder bone of the same deer attached to a piece of ash), a sharpening stone and a new necklace given to him by his mother to replace the one he had "lost." His mother also gave him a small pouch that contained several seeds of corn, squash and beans. What could he have forgotten to give me before I start my journey? he thought.

Little Hawk's father paused and pulled out a small turtle shell rattle. Small feathers wrapped in a threadlike material dangled from the handle. The shell itself was dull in color and very smooth. He had seen his father use it only on special occasions. He never knew the importance of this rattle or how his father ever got it. Rolling Thunder's eyes were filled with tears as he began to speak.

"Little Hawk," his father explained, "this rattle has been passed down from father to son for as long as anyone in our family can remember. My father handed it to me, and his father handed it to him. It gives me great pride to be able to hand this rattle to you."

Little Hawk was speechless. He didn't know what to say. He reached out and took the rattle and shook it softly.

"Use the rattle when you are in times of trouble," Rolling Thunder explained. "It will help calm your nerves, clear your mind and gain you entrance to the world of the spirits."

Little Hawk held the rattle in his right hand. He turned it over and back, gently rubbing each side. He thought of every member of his family who had held and owned it. Little Hawk's eyes welled with tears of pride, as he was so overcome with emotion that he couldn't speak. Tears wouldn't fall from his eyes, however, as he fought them back with all his might. Then he knelt down and gathered the items.

Little Hawk stepped out of the teepee, looked his father in the eye again and walked off into the early morning fog. He looked back only one time and the village was gone. The fog had completely swallowed his home. Now Little Hawk was completely alone. For the first time in his life, he had no one to rely on.

# 12

After walking all day, Little Hawk saw the sun was setting and decided to make camp. He ate some berries as he sat for the night. He built a fire and listened to it crackle as he thought of his family and the days ahead. After waking at dawn, Little Hawk walked another day, then thought of finding a place to live. He searched the forests to the east. There the land began to rise steeply and had many boulders deposited there from long ago, during a time they say that the land was covered with snow and ice. Little Hawk stumbled upon what would turn out to be the perfect spot. Two large rocks leaned on each other, creating a small opening between them. Sunlight came through a hole at the top of the cave, giving just enough light to see inside. The hole will serve another purpose, Little Hawk thought. It would act as an escape for the smoke from campfire. Little Hawk knew that the rocks around the fire in the village would still be warm long after the fire was out. He concluded that the rocks surrounding him would hold some of the heat from his fires. This could keep his new home warm if for some reason his fire died down or went out altogether.

Little Hawk set his belongings inside his new home and wasted no time getting to work. He went right away to gather tinder from the forest floor. This consisted of dried leaves, including pine needles, and dead grasses. He also gathered several small twigs and fallen branches to use as kindling. These were all kept in an area of the cave where they would not get wet. Little Hawk's next trip was to get larger pieces of wood to keep the fire going long into the night. He worked until he had a very large pile of wood stacked at the back of the cave.

Little Hawk took some of the dry tinder and placed it in a pile directly under the hole in the cave roof. He then took two small sticks, placing one on the ground and the other vertically, perpendicular to the stick on the ground. He placed his hands at the top of the vertical stick and rubbed his hands forward and back. At the same time, he moved his hands from the top of the stick to the bottom. He repeated this several times and before long smoke started to rise from the bottom stick. Little Hawk quickly placed some of the tinder around the smoke and repeated the same rubbing motion. More smoke filled the air. He put the sticks down and gently blew on the tinder. Soon flames appeared. Little Hawk added some of the dry twigs and fallen branches and gently blew at the base of the fire. Quickly flames rose high in the air. He waited for the twigs to become coals before adding the largest pieces of wood. The entire cave was aglow.

At this time, Little Hawk took a moment to observe his new surroundings. He was amazed to see the walls were covered with pictures, drawings of a single boy catching prey in a trap and hunting deer by a creek. There were other pictures of a boy skinning a deer and preparing the meat. He concluded that the images must have been created by someone just like him, a young boy going through his Seasons Away. Maybe this was the cave his father spoke of. Maybe these pictures were the ones his father drew.

Remembering what his father had taught him, Little Hawk studied the pictures closely. He thought that he could use the images to help find an area to set traps and hunt larger game. This was comforting. He thought this boy from the past could help lead the way and guide him over the next year.

With the sun almost disappearing below the horizon, Little Hawk searched the area for the roots of a small brushy tree. Knowing there was little light left in the day, he pulled the roots from the ground and with his knife quickly stripped off the bark. He tied the thin, rope-like material together. Once finished, he found the area in the forest that had been drawn on the wall of the cave. He quickly headed straight to the thickest gathering of briar bushes and shrubs. He could see a small path leading straight through the thickets and determined this is where he would place his trap. He made a small circle with the rope and tied the two loose ends to some small trees. The circle was only big enough for the head of a rabbit to fit through. When an unsuspecting rabbit traveled the path and stepped through the hole pushing forward, the rope would begin to tighten, holding the rabbit in place. The more the rabbit struggled, the tighter the rope would become.

Little Hawk set the trap, covered the rope with some leaves and small twigs and returned to the cave.

Upon arrival, with dwindling light, he made his way to the nearby creek in search of quality flat stones. These stones would be carefully converted into razor sharp arrowheads. His father had taught him that sharp bends in the creek were the perfect places to find such stones. During times of high water, the stones would be deposited where the creek turned. Then when the water subsided, the stones were left on dry ground.

Little Hawk had found several stones that were just the right thickness. He gathered them quickly. With the sun going down, he thought he would check on the trap he had set.

He approached the trap just as his uncle had taught him, stepping lightly so as not to make a sound. He was disappointed to see there was nothing in the snare. Just then there was movement in the bushes to his right. A large rabbit appeared and headed straight for the trap. Little Hawk watched as the rabbit approached the trap cautiously. It stepped through the hole and began to hop more quickly. The rope tightened around its shoulders. The more it tried to get free, the more ensnared it became.

Little Hawk darted from the bushes and in an instant the rabbit was dead. He began a verse that his grandfather, father and uncle had taught him. He praised the spirit of the rabbit. He gave thanks to that spirit for giving itself to him, completing an ancient ritual performed when any animal was taken.

The rabbit was cleaned and over the fire in no time. The hide of the rabbit was stretched to dry. Warm clothing would be needed for the harsh winter and the rabbit hide would make one half of a nice pair of moccasins. Little Hawk started working on the stones while the rabbit was being cooked. Finishing two stones, the rabbit was ready to be eaten. It was a fitting meal.

After eating, he took a leg bone from the rabbit and ground one end into a very sharp point. On the opposite end, he used his knife to poke a small hole. He made a needle for sewing his clothing in the future.

The light from the fire now dim, Little Hawk realized that he had been so consumed with building up his supplies that he had no time to think about being alone. He was prepared for almost every aspect of this challenge. His hunting and gathering skills were sharp. He could make or gather anything he needed. There was something he wasn't prepared for, however...the silence.

The village was always buzzing with people talking and walking about. Nights were filled with the elders telling stories of the past. Every evening the youngest members of the tribe would be dazzled by stories of their elders. Wild tales of hunts in the past as well as funny stories of the elders when they were children entertained not only the young but the older members as well.

Little Hawk remembered a particular story about his father. He was the slowest runner of all the boys. Most of the girls could beat him at a race as well. Everyone called him Keya, which meant the turtle. Keya was a word that was very important to their people. They identified thirteen months in a year because of the thirteen new moons. Each new moon consisted of twenty-eight days. Every twenty-eight days there would be a new moon, thus a new month. The turtle has thirteen different scales on its shell surface and also has twenty-eight small scales around the top of its shell. With these naturally occurring instances, the Keya or turtle became an important symbol to Little

Hawk's people.

The term they used for his father did not carry the same meaning, however. When members of the tribe would call him "Keya," they did it mockingly, teasing him because of his slowness. His legs were long and terribly thin, and his body was lean. No matter how he tried, he could not gather the coordination to put one foot in front of the other to move his body as fast as the other boys could. Little Hawk couldn't imagine his father being last at anything. But it was true. It wasn't until his Seasons Away that he gained the size, strength, coordination and confidence that he possessed today. After his Seasons Away, he never lost again. In fact, when he returned, no one would dare challenge him. Once he received his adult name, Rolling Thunder, not one person ever called him Keya again. Little Hawk's memory of his father at first made him smile. However, that happiness didn't last. He began to miss his father more and more.

Back in the village, as the members of the tribe dozed off to sleep, they would hum softly until their eyes were heavy and finally closed. He longed to hear a story, a voice humming softly in the night...something. He began to softly sing himself to sleep, but soon stopped. The singing made him sad. He felt as if there was an enormous empty hole in his chest. He tried to think of other funny stories the elders would tell, but it only made things worse. For the longest time he stared at the roof of the cave, holding back the tears of fear and loneliness. Finally, when his eyes became heavy, too heavy to hold open any longer, Little Hawk went to sleep, thus ending his first day away.

# 13

Little Hawk woke to the sound of birds chirping loudly outside his cave. He stood and stretched his arms high above his head. He rubbed the sleep from his eyes and looked at his surroundings. Slowly he made his way to the cave entrance and the sun warmed his face. It smiled down on him, letting Little Hawk know that this was going to be a beautiful spring day.

He was hungry and quickly snatched a piece of cornbread his mother made him and began to nibble. There was going to be a good deal of work for him in the beginning and Little Hawk was up to that challenge.

Little Hawk worked diligently to gather wood and supplies for his dwelling. He took the time to start turning the soil just outside his cave. He chose a spot where the grass was tall and already a rich dark green. Little Hawk knew the sun would shine the longest on this area and it would be a good place to plant his crops. He dug small holes and placed a seed of corn into the ground. With every seed that was placed in the ground, a small fish taken from the stream was also placed, helping the seed grow bigger and faster. Then the seed and small fish were softly covered with a layer of dirt. With dirt-covered hands, Little Hawk wiped the sweat from his brow and remembered his mother teaching him how to take smaller fish from the stream. She would step gently into the stream and actually herd the school of minnows into a shallow pool. There she would take a small net made from tightly woven grasses and scoop the fish out. Little Hawk laughed to himself as he remembered how good she was at taking these fish from the stream. He took small fish in the same manner as his mother.

Water was then carried and poured atop a small mound of dirt. Three rows of corn, squash and beans were planted. Little Hawk was confident each plant would grow and feed him during the winter. Realizing this was work done mainly by the women of the village didn't matter to Little Hawk during the Seasons Away. It was much tougher than he had imagined and he felt a new sense of respect for his mother and the other women of the tribe for doing such hard but necessary work.

As long as he was occupied with chores and preparing for the coming days, Little Hawk didn't feel a sense of being homesick. Time passed quickly, and the sun warmed his shoulders longer and longer with each passing day.

Early one late spring morning, Little Hawk was awakened by a loud rumbling sound. He was not alarmed, but the noise got him up and off his bed of soft pine needles quickly. He recognized this sound right away. It was the thunderous gobble of the male turkey. Walking quickly, Little Hawk grabbed his bow and quietly crept toward the entrance of the cave. There he waited until he heard it gobble again. Again, the turkey let out a holler. Little Hawk looked in the direction of the gobble and could see one large male in full strut about seventy-five yards from his dwelling.

Moving only when his prey would turn away to where its tail feathers would shield its vision, Little Hawk quickly shifted from tree to tree, drawing ever closer to the turkey. Finally, a large patch of blueberries was able to hide Little Hawk from the keen eyesight of the elusive long beard. Little Hawk cupped his left hand and turned his head. Then he made a chirping sound like that of a hen turkey. Immediately the male sounded off and turned in his direction. Little Hawk waited. After another gobble, he called again.

Boom! The turkey erupted! With every call, it walked in Little Hawk's direction. He could see the bird through tiny openings in the brush. After a few minutes, the turkey would be in perfect position for a shot. Little Hawk drew back his bow. The turkey stepped directly in front of the blueberry bush.

Snap!

The string jumped from his hand and the arrow traveled with incredible speed until it struck the bird just below its neck. Feathers flew as the turkey hopped into the air. The pierced turkey's body prevented it from running or flying away. Several female turkeys took to the air for a fast escape as Little Hawk darted from behind the bush to collect his bounty.

Knowing he could not eat the entire turkey in one meal, Little Hawk did with the turkey meat just what he had done with the deer and antelope meat. What he didn't cook, he cut into slivers and hung over the fire to make jerky.

The feathers delighted Little Hawk. The bright black and white colors of the wings stood in contrast to the deep rich brown and black of the tail feathers. Little Hawk's hair was growing longer and he braided one of each feather into his hair. The tail feather floated on top of his head and the wing feather dangled behind his ear. He looked at his reflection in the bowl of water near the fire and thought the feathers were fitting his personality as a growing young man.

The days were becoming long and hot. Even the nights were warm. Little Hawk knew it was time begin preparations for the winter, although it seemed so far away. He sat one morning and looked at his journal. He remembered something his father said so vividly, it was as if he was sitting beside him.

"Little Hawk," his father said, "you must realize that even though the days are warm and the sun stays long in the sky, soon it will be time for the birds to fly to their winter grounds and the animals to make their annual migration to warmer climates. The time to gather your things and prepare for the long cold winter is now. Do this and your time will not be difficult. If you don't, you may not survive your Seasons Away."

Each day would begin with Little Hawk tending his garden. He pulled the weeds that had grown around his plants. The corn had begun to shoot up and was already a few inches tall. If Little Hawk did not pull the weeds away, his plants would be overtaken and they wouldn't grow to their full potential. He knew the importance of these vegetables for his diet during his time of separation from the tribe. He was going to do everything in his power to ensure their proper growth.

Little Hawk then spent the rest of his time gathering supplies: wood to keep the fire going, flat stones for arrowheads, and berries from the forest to set out and dry. He gathered clay from the banks of the creek and carried it back to his cave. Little Hawk began to shape the wet clay into a bowl. It was smooth on the inside, as this was where the liquid would be placed. The outside of the bowl was not as important as the inside and often had a rough texture. He hung the bowl over the fire to make the clay hard and dry. It wasn't as good as ones his mother or sister could make, but the bowl would serve his purpose. Little Hawk made several bowls in different shapes and sizes. Some were for heating water over the fire. Others were for mashing corn to be baked into bread. And finally, some would be for holding the nuts and berries he would collect from the forest.

Little Hawk even remembered when his mother gathered small roots for flavoring water. He set out in search of the sassafras tree. Little Hawk pulled the roots and cleaned them in the nearby stream. He did as his mother did and placed them in a bowl of water that hung just above the coals of his fire. When steam began to rise from the surface, his drink was ready. He poured the hot drink into another cup-shaped bowl and slowly sipped it.

Little Hawk knew enough to keep track of where he found the tree and roots in his journal. When the weather turned cold and the ground became covered with snow, the landscape would look quite different. He could turn to his journal and find the area where the trees were without trouble.

Berries and small fruits were also every important for his diet. Blueberries, black raspberries and wild strawberries were all found on the forest floor. Many patches of these bushes were tracked and monitored by

Little Hawk. He knew that in late summer, they would start to turn color and be ready for eating.

In the village, the berries had many uses. They were used for eating as a light snack and were also dried and crushed into a powder to be added to meat. Yet another use was to squeeze the berries and drink the juice. The juice was even used to soothe a rough throat or to cure a harsh cough. Little Hawk was thankful he found several different patches that were loaded with these berries.

After studying the pictures on the cave wall, he set several traps along the creek banks. Every place where a trail was easily visible, Little Hawk placed a trap. These places were also drawn in the journal. He didn't want to end up like his father and be caught in one of his own traps.

Little Hawk was sure his time was being spent wisely. He had caught rabbits in the traps and taken antelope and deer on the edge of the forest with his bow and arrow. Each of these animals had an essential part in the harsh winter to come.

Many of the skins he had taken were stretched to dry properly and were now ready to be made into clothing. The rabbit's skins were made into moccasins for the winter. Their soft fur would be essential for keeping Little Hawk's feet warm when the snow fell.

Little Hawk did the same with the deer and antelope skins. They were made into leggings to cover his lower body and a shawl to wear over his shoulders. He also made blankets to keep himself warm throughout the long cold nights.

The berries were ripening nicely on the bushes but were not quite ready to be harvested. Everything was in perfect order for Little Hawk. He had plenty of food to eat, wood to burn and supplies to catch more food. His mind had been completely occupied with his preparations. He had no reason or time to think of others. Nights were getting easier as well. He found himself able to hum the songs of his people without becoming sad. The songs and the memories that were attached to them brought Little Hawk joy and he thought fondly of them once again. It was now much easier for him to fall asleep.

One morning Little Hawk was walking his regular trapline. There was something wrong, something very strange about one of the traps. The rope-like material had been snapped and the game was removed. There were no tracks from the animal that had taken the prey from the trap. This was confusing. Only a short distance down the trail he came across the carcass of an antelope. It was tucked neatly under a small pine tree covered with some leaves and other litter from the forest floor. He saw the huge tracks left in the dirt. Little Hawk knew right away what this meant...a grizzly!

He remembered everything his uncle told him about

the ferocious beast that roamed the forests. He knew the antelope was in storage. He also knew that at some point the bear would be back to feed on the carcass. He was very careful not to touch the dead animal. He didn't want to leave his scent anywhere near this kill. Slowly Little Hawk began to back away from the sight. Not looking where he was going, he stepped on a dried twig that had fallen from a tree branch above.

SNAP!

Little Hawk's eyes widened as he let everyone and everything in the forest know of his presence.

From behind a nearby shrub, Little Hawk heard a very low growl. It got louder, and the bushes began to shake. He couldn't move. His legs felt heavy with fear. Something was breathing down his neck. He could feel the hot breath of the beast blow his hair before his face. In an instant Little Hawk was knocked to the ground. Without looking up, he did just as his uncle had taught him to do. He curled into a ball, protecting his face and neck and pretended he was dead.

The animal circled him several times and stopped. There was a long silence. Not a bird overhead or a chipmunk scurrying along the ground could be heard. Then a hideous sounding laugh pierced Little Hawk's ears.

Running Bear.

He had banded together with Tiny Beaver and

Muskrat, which was against the rules of the tribe. The Seasons Away was to be spent alone. It was a rite of passage into manhood, to survive and find oneself.

Little Hawk opened his eyes and tried to get to his feet. With that attempt, he was knocked back to the ground. Just as before, they came at him all at once and began to kick at Little Hawk. They punched and poked. They stopped only for an instant, but it was enough for Little Hawk to spring to his feet. He crouched and was ready to fight.

"Look at this, would ya!" Running Bear said with surprise.

"Leave me alone!" Little Hawk shouted at the three boys. "I'll take you all out!"

The threat didn't work. Tiny Beaver and Muskrat both ran at Little Hawk at the same time. He couldn't decide which one to hit and which to avoid. He couldn't move to his left or his right. He froze. The two collided into Little Hawk at exactly the same time, sending him to the forest floor. Muskrat stood over him, one foot on the ground and the other planted squarely on Little Hawk's chest, pinning him to the ground. Running Bear knelt down beside Little Hawk.

"The rabbit was good!" Running Bear said with a sneer.

"We were getting hungry," Muskrat said as he stared down.

"You!" Little Hawk said quietly under his breath.

"What were you thinking, Little Hawk? You can't stand up to us," Running Bear scolded Little Hawk and ripped the turkey feather from atop his head.

The others laughed villainously at Little Hawk and slipped away into the brush. Running Bear shook his head in disgust, then vanished as well.

Little Hawk thought he wouldn't have to deal with them during this time away. He thought that they would be more concerned with surviving than with picking on him. He thought they would follow the rules and grow into respectful young men. Nothing was further from the truth. What a way to spend the next year, alone dealing with the wild and trying to avoid Running Bear!

Little Hawk had been so startled by the run-in that he had forgotten to tell them about the bear and the antelope carcass. Little Hawk thought he should warn the boys that a grizzly was in the area and that it had an antelope stored under the tree. He was too stunned to remember to tell them. They were all in danger.

Little Hawk determined that if the trio was too ignorant to realize that there was a bear in the area, it would be their own demise. He went back to his dwelling. He continued working on what he needed to make it through his rite of passage.

The next morning, while again walking the trapline, Little Hawk noticed the antelope carcass was gone. Did the bear return and move it to a different location? Little Hawk thought. Then he saw the drag marks and footprints left in the dirt. It had to be Running Bear and the others. "This is the worst thing they could have done," Little Hawk whispered to himself. He began to follow the drag marks but quickly stopped. He didn't want to be anywhere near this scene for fear the bear would return and think he was the one who had stolen its meal.

Clouds gathered in the sky. Rain soon began to fall, so Little Hawk thought it would be best to stay in the cave and continue working on other articles of clothing. The wind blew softly and the rain gently fell all day and most of the night. He sat in the cave and looked at the pictures in his journal while eating pieces of deer jerky. Occasionally, lightning would light up the entrance of the cave, followed by a low rumbling of thunder. The fire gave a soft glow and cast a shadow on the wall that held some of the drawings. He stood and stared at his own shadow for a few minutes. He could see the outline of the feathers in his hair and thought himself fierce. He pretended his shadow was Running Bear, Muskrat or Tiny Beaver. He threw punches at the shadow. He pretended the shadow fought back and tried to avoid their attacks. He could see it all happening in his mind. Little Hawk would defeat all three and finally gain their respect. After a time, Little Hawk was out of breath.

Finally, he retired for the night. He lay on his right side and stared at the fire, thinking of the bear. He hoped that it would not realize that those boys stole its meal. He didn't want any harm to come to them. Little Hawk imagined what a bear attack might feel like. The pain would be unbearable, he thought. The thoughts made him shiver.

# 14

Little Hawk was getting tired of eating the same old meat each day. He was always thankful for the meat he had but wanted something a little different. Fish! Maybe he would try to take some fish from the stream. Walking along the banks, checking his traps, he always noticed large trout darting for the cover of the banks as he strolled by. He thought he would try something new.

The following day, Little Hawk rose at dawn and headed for the stream. On the banks of the creek, Little Hawk chose a long straight sapling to use. Within an hour, he had transformed the sapling into a lightning fast piercing spear. The sapling was stripped of all its bark and the point was intricately carved with small barbs and hooks for holding onto its prey.

He walked softly along the banks of the creek, looking for a small pool where a fish would likely be. He went only a few yards and there they were. Several native brook trout were gathered in the hole. Cautiously Little Hawk approached the pool. Some of the trout darted under the safety of the bank. He froze. Holding the same position for a few minutes, the fish returned to the center of the pool. Slowly Little Hawk raised his spear and with hardly a splash it plunged into the water. On his first attempt he had...NOTHING. When the water cleared, the fish were nowhere to be found. The second and third attempts in nearby holes rendered the same results...NOTHING. His stomach started to rumble with hunger.

Discouraged and still wanting something new to eat, Little Hawk returned to the cave. He sat beside the fire pit, where a few bits of log were still smoldering, and referenced his journal. He opened to the part about fishing. He looked at the pictures and thought, When spearing a fish, the spear must enter the water a short distance in front of the fish. The water makes the fish appear farther away than it actually is.

Feeling a renewed sense of confidence, he returned to the stream. The spear raised above his shoulder and SPLASH. When Little Hawk pulled the spear from the water, he was delighted to see a struggling trout pierced through the middle and held fast.

The next few holes, Little Hawk experienced the same success. He caught only enough fish to eat for one meal at a time. He never let anything he killed go to waste.

The fish taken in this manner were different from

the smaller minnows taken to plant with the seeds. These fish would be for placing over the fire and eating. These were different from the fish that would act as a fertilizer and help the corn grow faster.

Days went by quickly as Little Hawk spent much of the time checking and setting traps, making arrows and arrowheads and gathering enough supplies for the fire. Many nights were spent working to turn ordinary skins into articles of clothing for the coming winter.

On a night that the temperature dipped sharply, Little Hawk was studying the pictures on the cave wall and noticed a number of slash marks. They were all grouped together. Each group had twenty-eight marks in them. He quickly realized that each group represented a new moon. There was a new moon every twenty-eight days. He thought the boy who made them must have been keeping track of the days by making the marks on the wall. He counted all the marks. There were 364.

Not wanting to confuse the marks that he would make, Little Hawk scratched a line separating the new from the old. He also drew a picture of himself beside the marks. He sat back staring at them and then turned in for the night.

As the time passed quickly, Little Hawk noticed his bow was easier and easier to pull back. The string would not reach his face anymore. The arrows weren't flying as fast or as far. Even the handle of the bow wasn't fitting properly in the palm in his hand. His hands were much too large. He needed a new bow, a larger bow.

He remembered the lessons his father had taught him and followed every step. His journal was well organized with pictures of everything necessary for making a precision arrow-launching weapon. Little Hawk had prepared the sinew for the string. It was all ready to go. Now his bow.

The sapling was chosen. It was a dark colored ash tree that, when stripped of its bark, revealed a very interesting grain pattern. A mineral had been absorbed into the tree and discolored one of the age rings. Little Hawk knew that it was perfect to make his bow. After a few days of carving and smoothing rough edges with a coarse stone, his bow was ready. He applied several pieces of sinew, each one smaller than the one before. After a few days more, the bow was finished.

An old ant ridden stump was just to the east end of the cave entrance. Little Hawk thought this would be a great target to practice with his new bow and arrows. On the north end of the stump grew a large mushroom. He picked it and placed in on the side of the stump, using the stem of the mushroom to hold it in place. Little Hawk stepped backwards ten paces. He pulled an arrow from his quiver and nocked it on his string. He drew the arrow back to his cheek, with the bow leaning slightly. He released the arrow from the bow. It traveled through the air more quickly than Little Hawk had ever seen an arrow fly.

SMACK! It hit the center of the mushroom with such force it blew the mushroom into tiny pieces and embedded the arrow halfway up its shaft. Little Hawk was pleased. He didn't need to take another practice shot. His bow was ready.

Now that Little Hawk was confident he had stockpiled enough supplies, he sat back one evening to reflect of the first two months of his independence. The sun began to fall below the horizon when he heard the sound of a wolf howling in the distance. The howls and growls became louder and louder. He grabbed his bow, nocked an arrow and crept slowly to the cave entrance. He cautiously inspected the area around his home. He found nothing. Little Hawk went back inside and fell asleep. During the night, strange sounds were heard outside the cave and awakened him. Little Hawk became alarmed. The fire was nearly out, giving almost no light. His eyes were wide, trying to catch any movement at the cave entrance. Again he saw nothing. Little Hawk stoked the fire and spent the rest of the night awake, listening to the eerie sounds in the distance and clutching his bow tightly.

Morning light finally came. "That was the longest night of my life!" Little Hawk said aloud. He walked outside to examine the tracks of the animal that had kept him awake. He searched almost the entire morning and found no tracks. He thought he would find the signs of the wolf or maybe a mountain lion. Then he thought of the grizzly and the antelope carcass. He expected to find the grizzly's tracks. What he found was a path with no fresh tracks on it whatsoever. "What could have made so much noise but leave no tracks behind?" Little Hawk asked himself, puzzled.

He quickly went inside the cave and opened his journal. He turned to the part about tracking and hunting. He could find nothing about an animal being clever enough to cover its own tracks. Maybe last night was a dream, he thought to himself. Then he realized how exhausted he was from not sleeping. He knew it was real. Confused, Little Hawk sat his journal down and went on with his daily chores.

Strange sounds were again heard off and on throughout the following nights. Different sounds. Little Hawk couldn't recognize them distinctly. Sometimes they sounded wolf-like. Sometimes like a coyote. These sounds baffled him.

One night, Little Hawk went in search of the animal that would make such strange noises. He waited until the moon was full and there were no clouds overhead. The moon gave off enough light to enable Little Hawk to see through the forest and fields.

A bark! Then a short howl came from the top of the

next low ridge. Little Hawk hustled through the valley and up the other side. He was breathing heavily and had to slow his breath so he could listen for something walking through the woods. He waited. His breath slowed. Another bark followed by a yip. Where could they be? he thought. Little Hawk nocked an arrow as he felt the makers of the sounds were close by. He walked silently. When he arrived at the spot where he thought the animals would be, they were gone. He made several short barking sounds himself, hoping that the animals would bark back at him. Only the sound of a screeching owl broke the silence of the night.

Little Hawk made his way back through the forest and across an open field leading to his dwelling. He walked inside the cave and drank from a small cup filled with fresh water.

Things were moving smoothly. Many moons came and went. Supplies were gathered, food was prepared and clothes were made. There were many markings on the wall now, so many that he had forgotten about Running Bear and the others. The days were becoming shorter and the nights colder. One evening Little Hawk could see his breath in the air. The Seasons Away was going very well. Or at least he thought. He was confident in his abilities, but still nagging at him was the thought of a difficult time where he was to make an arduous decision.

As a hindquarter of a deer cooked over the fire, its hide stretched out and drying, a loud noise startled Little Hawk. He jumped to his feet, clutching his knife in his left hand. His bow was not in reach. A large grumbling growl came from outside the cave. The snarling and growling became louder as the beast neared the cave entrance. One thought rushed through Little Hawk's mind...GRIZZLY! The great grizzly that had haunted his dreams for as long as he could remember was now at his doorstep.

Little Hawk crept slowly toward the back of the cave. His hands trembled with fear. He felt the back wall of the cave and knew there was no place to go and nowhere to hide. He remembered what his uncle and father had taught him when facing a grizzly...play dead. Little Hawk fell to his knees, then onto his side, protecting his vital areas, his neck and chest. This was the only way to survive an attack. He closed his eyes and hoped the beast would leave him alone. His thoughts quickly shifted to the deer leg cooking over the fire. If the beast were hungry enough, maybe it would take the meat over the fire and be gone.

Then it entered the cave. Little Hawk's palms were dripping with sweat as he lost the grip of his knife and it fell to the cave floor. His heart was pounding so hard against his chest he thought for sure the beast would see it.

Something wasn't right. There was more than one...
WOLVES! Little Hawk didn't know how to confront
wolves. How many are there? Were these the ones
making the noises so long ago on the ridge? he thought.
The only thing to do was remain motionless on the floor
of the cave.

Several strips of jerky were also hanging to dry and
Little Hawk hoped that would be enough to satisfy their
hunger and spare his life. The footsteps came closer
and Little Hawk could feel the dust kicked up from
the cave floor settle on his face as the animals walked
closely by. Then complete silence. Everything was still.
Little Hawk opened one eye slightly to see what was
happening.

"Look what we have here, boys," a familiar but
unsettling voice said. "What a coward!" The others
laughed. They weren't wolves! It was Running Bear,
Tiny Beaver and Muskrat.

"Quite the place you have here!" Running Bear said.
"Not a bad place at all." As Running Bear spoke, Tiny
Beaver and Muskrat helped themselves to some meat
from above the fire. After taking a large bite, Tiny Beaver
tossed the leg of deer to Running Bear. He caught the
leg and began to gorge himself. Helplessly, Little Hawk
remained on the cave floor. Running Bear wiped the
juice dripping from his chin. He grabbed Little Hawk
by the hair and lifted him to his feet. "What else do you

have for us?" Running Bear asked.

"Nothing? Did you not learn how to fend for yourself? Did anyone teach you?" Little Hawk asked.

"We learned to fend for ourselves. And we're doing it. Thanks for helping out!" Running Bear said with a sneer.

"What do you mean?"

"With you around, we don't need to hunt, fish or make anything. That's your job!" Running Bear replied sternly.

All the while, Muskrat was rummaging through Little Hawk's things. He held up the pouch holding arrowheads, needles and a necklace. He also held up arrows, a bow and dried skins already made into articles of clothing. And last but not least he pointed to a large pouch of jerky.

"I've worked very hard on those! What am I to do without them?" said Little Hawk.

"Don't know and don't care!" replied Running Bear.

Little Hawk stepped backward and crouched into a position, showing Running Bear he was ready to defend his home and belongings. Running Bear laughed, and the others joined in, mocking Little Hawk.

"Still, you haven't learned?" Running Bear asked, almost in disbelief. He shook his head, then nodded at Muskrat, sending him to attack. Little Hawk slid to his left and stepped out of the way of Muskrat's punch.

He pulled Muskrat's arm forward at the same time and sent him stumbling to the ground. Tiny Beaver looked surprised and in an instant rushed Little Hawk. This time Little Hawk slipped to his right and landed a shot to the midsection of Tiny Beaver, leaving him gasping for breath as he lay on the floor of the cave.

Running Bear was furious, mainly at the fruitless attempts to bring Little Hawk down. "You fools!" Running Bear yelled. "At the same time!"

He demanded they try again. Just as before, Little Hawk brushed them aside. Eventually Little Hawk became tired, too tired to fight them off.

Soon Tiny Beaver and Muskrat together were able to subdue him. With the two of them holding his arms behind his back, Running Bear slugged Little Hawk in the stomach. That blow took his breath and dropped him to his knees. Running Bear bent down and lifted Little Hawk's chin. "You've become a bit more courageous, Chicken Hawk, but not brave enough!" Little Hawk felt a thud against his cheek. Then everything went black.

When he came to, his home was destroyed. He only had three items left, his knife, his journal, and his rattle.

With his cheek and left eye swollen and throbbing, Little Hawk started a fire and began to straighten up his living quarters. Scraps of food were dropped on the cave floor, as Running Bear and the others were careless when leaving the cave. Little Hawk gathered up what he could, a few strips of meat and some nuts and dried berries. He slept very little the next few nights. Every twig that snapped outside the cave startled him. The slightest noise and he was up.

After a few days, the fear began to fester inside him. And soon it grew into anger, a hatred that he had never felt before. The feeling now consumed him. As each day passed, Little Hawk spent more and more time replaying the events in his mind. With every memory, the hatred grew. He became enraged and decided to take back his things and more importantly, his respect.

I will separate them! he thought. Finally, when Running Bear is alone, I will attack!

He sat close to the fire and began to crush the berries he had collected from the forest. He could hear the drums of the village beating in his head as if they were pounding right beside him. Little Hawk could see the intense look on the faces of the braves as they prepared for their battle. His eyes became cold and distant. He began to color his own face just as they did with red and black paint. He chanted the songs he had heard the men in the village chant. He felt as if he was floating in the air, watching himself prepare for his own battle. He gently put the bowl on the cave floor and stood up. Little Hawk caught a glimpse of his reflection in the water in another small bowl. He had never looked so fierce!

Luckily for Little Hawk, it hadn't rained for quite some time. Tracking the three hoodlums would be very easy. When evening fell, he made a fire but didn't sleep. He thought more and more of the plan to confront Running Bear.

"It would have to be a surprise, an ambush," he thought. "I must take them one by one, when they least expect it." He went over the plan several times in his head.

The next morning, he was already moving at dawn. He was again replaying the attack and was fully enraged when he noticed something very strange about the path. Bear tracks, large bear tracks! A grizzly. It appeared to be following the tracks of the boys. Little Hawk's rage was immediately gone. The only thought in his head was to somehow warn Running Bear. He and the others were in grave danger.

But what if he doesn't believe me? Then his thoughts shifted. "Maybe the bear should attack them. They would get exactly what they deserve!"

Those thoughts quickly left Little Hawk's head. They are my brothers! I must warn them!

Little Hawk ran as fast as he could, still following the tracks of the bear. Over fallen trees, across large boulders, he moved swiftly. He traveled as fast as his legs could carry him. The trail ended at the top of a ridge with a very steep drop-off. A small path winding down the hillside. Little Hawk stood at the top of the ridge and peered over the edge. What he saw was shocking. Running Bear was pinned against a large bolder with nowhere to run. The great grizzly, only a few yards away, snarled and pawed at the ground.

Running Bear begged his friends to help him. Tiny Beaver and Muskrat were frozen stiff with fear. The bear didn't bother with them. Running Bear was its target.

"Please help me!" he screamed to them. They looked at each other, then at the bear and back to each other. At first, fear had their legs glued to the ground. But then they realized they could only make one choice...RUN! And run they did. They ran as fast as they could. They did not think of anyone's fate but their own.

Muskrat was looking back at the bear and tripped over a root, dropping the bow and quiver full of arrows that he'd taken from Little Hawk. He stumbled and fell to the ground. Muskrat was sure the bear would be on him, but it never took its eyes off Running Bear. He got to his feet and was into the brush, gone in an instant. He ran behind a large tree and stopped to catch his breath. He leaned back with his shoulders against the tree, chest heaving, eyes closed. Mukrat heard the screams of his friend as the bear began to draw closer. His eyes instantly popped open and he took off again.

He jumped over a stream and landed hard on a rock that turned his ankle badly. Driven by adrenaline,

Muskrat kept going. He had no idea the damage he was causing his body. He wanted to get as far away as he could. Over logs and through the briar patches he ran. His body was scratched and torn badly.

Little Hawk on the other hand, watched from high on the ridge as the bear closed in. He thought to himself that if Running Bear played dead, the grizzly might leave him. Instead, Running Bear screamed at his so-called friends, "COWARDS!" He tried to defend himself, throwing whatever rocks he could find. Running Bear grabbed a large stick off the ground, crouched and began stabbing the air wildly and yelling, hoping to deter the beast.

As the large grizzly was focused on Running Bear, Little Hawk slipped down the ridge and grabbed his bow and quiver of arrows. He quickly got into position. Little Hawk was only a few yards away when the bear struck.

The great grizzly raised its mighty paw and with one swipe, Running Bear's face was torn open. Huge gashes ran from his hairline above his left eye, across his cheek, and ended below his chin. Blood streamed down his chest and onto the ground as he fell. He stumbled to his feet as the bear clamped down on his leg, crushing the bone inside. Running Bear screamed in agony. The bear released him. His body went limp and his vision became blurry. Running Bear thought the end was near. Something moved at the bottom of the bluff. He could hear the beast breathing loudly as it stood over him. Then the loudest and most terrifying roar he had ever heard echoed through the forest, and everything went black.

Little Hawk stood, drew an arrow and placed it directly into the bear's ribs. The bear wheeled around, pulling at the arrow with his teeth. Little Hawk had never heard such a terrible scream from an animal. He quickly drew another arrow and sunk it into the bear's neck.

The great grizzly turned, spotted Little Hawk in the brush, and started after him. The bear stood on its hind legs directly in front of him, bleeding badly from the neck and chest, its paw raised, ready to swipe. At first Little Hawk froze. This was his dream all over again! The paw, the teeth, the dripping saliva...the dream flashed before his eyes. Then quickly Little Hawk pulled the last of the arrows from the quiver. He only had time to draw back and release. No aiming was necessary as the giant bear was practically on top of him. The arrow jumped from the string and deeply penetrated the bear's chest, piercing its heart. The bear fell, knocking Little Hawk to the ground. He got quickly to his feet but stumbled backward. He stared at the giant animal. It made one final attempt to strike Little Hawk as it lunged forward but didn't have enough life left to do any damage. One last paw raised and then fell harmlessly to the ground.

The giant bear took its last breath and expired.

Little Hawk stared in awe as blood slowly trickled from its nostrils. His first thought was of the vision he had of the bear, the nightmare he had since childhood. He couldn't believe that it had actually happened! The bear from the vision had a tear in its left ear, as did this one. Grandfather was right, he thought. Visions do help guide the future!

Little Hawk placed the bow beside the enormous bear. He looked at the giant with remorse. He recited the ancient verse to show respect to the bear and its spirit. He did not intend to kill the bear. He only wanted to get ahead of it so that he could warn the three boys. Killing the great beast was only in self-defense.

His thoughts quickly turned to Running Bear. He sprinted to his collapsed body and feared the worst. As Running Bear lay in a puddle of his own blood, Little Hawk felt his neck for a pulse and listened for any sign of breathing. Running Bear's breath gurgled as the blood from his face filled his mouth. Little Hawk first stopped the bleeding from his face and leg. Then he picked him up and carried him the entire way back to the cave. He had to stop several times to rest, as carrying Running Bear was not an easy task.

Upon arrival at the cave, Little Hawk took a large piece of hide and quickly stripped off the hair. He soaked it in a bowl of water that was heated over the fire. When the hide was soft, he pulled it from the water. After doing his best to straighten Running Bear's fractured leg, Little Hawk wrapped the soft hide around the upper thigh area and quickly sewed it together. When the material would cool and dry out, it would shrink, holding the damaged part of Running Bear's leg in place, helping it to heal.

Little Hawk made sure all cuts and puncture wounds were no longer bleeding and covered them with a small wrapping. Not wanting to waste any time, he quickly made his way back to the giant bear. Little Hawk struggled to separate the hide from the carcass. He rolled the hide into a ball, tucking the enormous head and paws inside.

Next Little Hawk worked diligently to quarter the animal. He threw one large hindquarter over his shoulder and made the trek back to the cave. He placed the leg and hide inside and returned to the body. After three exhausting trips, Little Hawk had everything back to the cave. There was no time to rest. He went right to work on the hide, turning it so that the fleshy side was exposed to the air. Using a ground shoulder bone of an antelope, Little Hawk began to scrape away the fat and blood sticking to the underside of the bear cape. He stretched and pinned the hide to the ground using small wooden stakes he carved.

He then placed large chunks of meat into a bowl of

water and hung it over the fire. Other meat was cut into strips for drying and smoking. Finally, Little Hawk kept much of the fat from the bear to rub on his skin. This would help to keep pesky insects such as mosquitos and ticks off his body. When all this was done, Little Hawk then turned his attention back to Running Bear.

He did the best he could with what supplies he had left in his cave. However, Little Hawk knew that if he didn't get different medicine, Running Bear would surely die. The medicine I need is in the village, he thought. But if I return, I will be banished from the tribe forever.

His thoughts went back and forth for quite some time. Running Bear was still unconscious, but Little Hawk could somehow sense he was in great pain.

He needed advice. He wanted to talk with his father and uncle but knew he couldn't. This was the hardest decision of his life. Running Bear was placed close to the fire. Little Hawk couldn't understand how Running Bear could be so cold yet covered with sweat at the same time. He walked outside the cave and was greeted by an owl that landed on a branch overhead. He remembered that the owl meant he would have wisdom when making a difficult decision. The owl circled and then flew to a nearby branch. Little Hawk didn't know why, but he felt as though he should follow. He walked until the owl perched on a low hanging limb of a beech tree. At the foot of the tree, Little Hawk found a plant he needed to help him enter the spirit world.

Quickly, he dug up the roots. Little Hawk returned to the cave and in no time was mixing the root with another secret ingredient. He desperately needed the help of his ancestors. Little Hawk knew they would not lead him astray.

Within minutes, the drink was ready. Little Hawk took two huge gulps and dropped the cup on the floor. It was the worst tasting drink he ever had. It was so bad that he thought he did something wrong. Many times, he had watched the elders in his tribe make the potion and he followed the same steps exactly as they had done. They had taken the drink and not even made as much as a strange face.

Little Hawk sat closely by the fire, shaking the small turtle shell rattle. The soft sound of the beads inside the rattle and the faint crackling of the fire were all Little Hawk could hear. He began to hum softly the songs he had heard his grandfather and other elders in the tribe sing. His vision blurred. He looked at his hands shaking the rattle and things started to change. The cave he sat in started to spin and he became dizzy.

Soon, a fog began to enter the cave and it was hard for Little Hawk to see. He stopped shaking the rattle, stood and started to walk through the mist and out of the cave. The territory seemed to be unfamiliar to him, but he sensed calmness. Little Hawk felt comfortable. He began to see figures appear right out of the mist. Their faces became clear and they seemed happy to see him.

As he walked through this strange place, the people were all sitting and smiling happily as he strolled by. He tried to talk to them. He needed answers! No one spoke. He watched as several groups worked together on hides to clean and prepare them for their intended use. The strangest thing was that not one person here was speaking. Each was just working to help the other members of the group to get the hides done. He walked from group to group, asking why he should help Running Bear when he caused him so much pain. "I have lived in fear my whole life because of him!" he said to them.

A few old women stopped what they were doing and raised their arms and pointed across the way. Little Hawk saw a group of children. He watched as they worked, played and took turns without as much as a cross-look between them. Little Hawk knew exactly what this meant. He knew that Running Bear, despite having caused him so much pain in his life, was a brother and needed his help. A very small, old woman approached Little Hawk and whispered gently into his ear, "It is time for you to return Little Hawk."

As the words trickled into his ear, the fog began to roll in again. The people began to make their way into the mist. They all nodded and smiled to Little Hawk and then were gone. He wanted to follow them, but his legs wouldn't carry him in their direction. He was left alone once again. He began to feel sick and sat on the ground, placing his head between his knees. With a heavy sweat dripping from his forehead, he stood quickly and found himself standing beside the fire in his cave. He bolted to the entrance of the cave and bent over, vomiting violently as his stomach cramped.

He stood straight again. "I have to!" Little Hawk said aloud. "He is my brother!" The thought of the children working together was burned into his memory. He glanced up and saw the owl leave the branch and head in the direction of the tribe.

He knew the risk he was taking, but also realized there was no other choice. He must return to the village and get the medicine to save Running Bear's life.

# 15

Under the cover of darkness, Little Hawk slipped into the village. He headed specifically into the medicine man's teepee. He was asleep.

Little Hawk crept quietly inside and gathered exactly what he needed to help his injured brother. With his arms full of supplies, Little Hawk couldn't balance everything and dropped several items. He froze! The medicine man rolled over. Little Hawk thought he was caught for sure.

The medicine man rolled back on his side. Little Hawk quickly gathered what he had dropped and headed for his cave. He traveled all night, as quickly as he could, being careful not to spill or drop any of the essential medicine. He applied some of the ointments to the cuts and puncture wounds on Running Bear's body. His father told him that it would help prevent infection.

He forced a liquid potion into Running Bear's mouth. He was also told this would help with the pain and keep him asleep.

Little Hawk kept him close to the fire and kept

him covered with warm blankets for several days. During this time, Little Hawk thought of nothing but Running Bear's condition. He kept the fire going throughout the night.

One evening, Running Bear began to sweat. His body was dripping wet. His forehead was hot to the touch. Little Hawk feared the worst. He thought this was the end. That night he stayed by Running Bear's side until he was too exhausted to keep his eyes open and fell asleep.

When he awoke the next morning, he was surprised to see Running Bear staring at him. He rubbed his eyes and looked again. Sure enough, Running Bear was awake.

Everything at first was blurry for Running Bear. His surroundings weren't familiar. He tried to focus on the person across the fire. A voice said, "Here drink this. It will help you sleep." He felt a bowl touch his lip and did as the voice suggested. Before he knew it, he was asleep again.

Finally, after many days, Running Bear was awake and could see clearly. His eyes were fixed on the person next to him. The boy's back was turned to Running Bear. "How did I get here? Is this real or am I dreaming?" he asked.

"You're not dreaming," the boy across the fire said. "I carried you here and gave you medicine. I went back to the tribe at night and took the medicine. Without it, you...well never mind that. How do you feel?" The person turned, and Running Bear saw for the first time it was Little Hawk!

"YOU! Why...why did you help me? After everything that has happened, after everything I did to you. You could have been banished if you were caught in the village."

"I know what would have happened had I been caught, but I wasn't. You are my brother and you were in trouble. I had to. I had no choice," said Little Hawk in a stern voice. "I looked to the spirits of our ancestors and they gave me direction."

Running Bear was quiet for some time. Then he spoke again. "I have to be honest with you. Before this, I don't know if I would have made the same decision you did."

"Quiet now," Little Hawk said. "Finish what is in your bowl. You need your rest. You need your strength. We will talk later."

Running Bear swallowed the remainder of the mixture that was in the bowl and quickly fell asleep.

Little Hawk took this time to reflect on what had happened. He had saved the life of the person who caused him the most pain, he had killed an animal that he truly did not want to kill and then had broken the number one rule of the Seasons Away. He returned to the tribe! Is this the "wise" decision I was to make? Little Hawk thought.

He walked to the outside of the cave while Running Bear slept and proceeded to remove all the claws from the bearskin. Next, using a leg bone from a rabbit that had been ground to a sharp point, he drilled a small hole at the top of each claw. When each was ready, Little Hawk cut a sliver of deer hide and strung the claws together. When finished, he had made the grandest of necklaces he had ever seen. He fancied the necklace as it reminded him of the courage it took to down the great beast.

Little Hawk slipped the necklace over his head and rubbed his fingers over the large claws. He walked back in the cave and sat next to Running Bear as he slept.

# 16

When Running Bear finally woke, he struggled to his feet, but could not stand. He crawled his way to the entrance of the cave. There he sat quietly and watched Little Hawk work on the large bearskin. The underside of the hide was completely clean of meat, fat or blood. He was working on the hide, stretching it to dry. A large chunk of meat hung over the fire and many smaller strips of meat hung to dry.

Running Bear reached down and felt the hard, leathery hide that was wrapped tightly around his leg. He had never seen anything like it. He was amazed at what Little Hawk knew how to do. He was seeing an entirely different side of Little Hawk for the first time. He wasn't timid, weak or shy. He had grown. He was strong, confident and courageous.

"How long have I been down?" Running Bear finally spoke.

"It has been many moons since the encounter with the great bear," Little Hawk replied.

"How many?" he asked again.

Little Hawk walked to the back of the cave and counted the marks on the wall. "Twenty-two to be exact," Little Hawk answered.

"What about Muskrat and Tiny Beaver?" The questions kept coming.

Little Hawk said, "I haven't seen them since the night of the attack."

"We must find them and help them!" Running Bear insisted.

"I have been so focused on you and your health, I had forgotten about them," Little Hawk said earnestly. "Where do you think they would be after so many days?"

"I will take you to them," Running Bear replied. He struggled and tried to get to his feet. He could put no pressure on his injured leg and in trying to stand his head began to throb.

He thumped back to a seated position. Not being discouraged, Running Bear tried again, but still couldn't stand. Running Bear then rolled onto his side, hoping to use the momentum to get to his feet. Again, he failed.

"You are not strong enough," said Little Hawk. "Tell me where they are and I'll bring them here."

Catching his breath, Running Bear explained in detail exactly where the boys would be. He knew they couldn't survive much longer without any food. Water was plentiful, but their ability to catch and clean prey was very poor. "Once they had eaten everything we took from you, they will be hungry. They wouldn't know how to ration that food and make it last."

"I shall go and bring them back. When we return, we will eat and talk," said Little Hawk.

He started down the path in search of Muskrat and Tiny Beaver. Running Bear was sure they would go back to what they knew. He thought the boys would return to the site where they had been for the past few months. He was right. Running Bear had directed Little Hawk directly to them.

Muskrat and Tiny Beaver were huddled together. They hadn't eaten anything substantial in nearly a month. Their faces were thin and drawn. Each had lost a considerable amount of weight. Muskrat could put little weight on his ankle. It was severely swollen and was the color of the sky before a heavy rain. The discoloration had covered the entire outside of his foot and had started to creep up his leg.

Little Hawk approached the two boys and they flinched in fear, not knowing if he was there to help or harm them. Little Hawk took two small pieces of dried meat from his pouch and handed one piece to each boy. They nearly swallowed the meat whole.

I doubt they even tasted it, Little Hawk thought.

Little Hawk gave them each another piece and said that was all they would get for a little while. Because they hadn't eaten in a very long time, they needed to eat small portions at first.

"We'll make camp here tonight and then we will all return to the cave in the morning," said Little Hawk.

"We?" asked Tiny Beaver.

"Yes," answered Little Hawk. "We are all brothers. We will return in the morning."

"Can we do that?" asked Tiny Beaver. "Isn't that against the rules?"

"Now you are worried about rules?" Little Hawk asked sarcastically.

"What of Running Bear?" asked Muskrat. "Is he..."

"He is fine. I will take you to him in the morning."

Little Hawk asked if the boys had any of the things they had taken from him. Tiny Beaver and Muskrat looked confused.

"Any rawhide, or skins, anything?" he asked.

Tiny Beaver handed over a piece of skin they had thrown in the corner, not knowing how to turn it into clothing. Little Hawk instructed Tiny Beaver to go to the stream and gather some water. He did. He brought the water back and Little Hawk began to heat it over the fire. Soon he was soaking skin in the hot water. After some time, Little Hawk pulled the skin out and wrapped it tightly around Muskrat's swollen ankle. He screamed as the skin was hot and his ankle still so sensitive. Little Hawk sewed the ends together.

"When it cools, it will shrink and harden. It will help you to walk in the morning," Little Hawk said sincerely. "You will still have pain, but at least you will be able to walk to the cave."

Little Hawk handed the boys a final piece of meat and then built a small fire. He left the location to gather some larger wood to keep the fire going into the night. He noticed the boys whispering to each other. His first thoughts were that they were planning another attack on him, that they would wait and become healthy enough to steal everything that he had, again!

That night, Little Hawk barely slept. My life would be so much easier if I had let them deal with their own fate, he thought. But soon, those thoughts vanished as he was exhausted and drifted off to sleep.

Morning came, and they were set to begin the journey back to the cave. Little Hawk had given Muskrat a stick almost as tall as he was. At the top was a place where the stick branched out. He had taken a piece of hide and tied it over the "y" of the stick and placed it under Muskrat's shoulder.

"Put you weight on the stick and it will help you walk," said Little Hawk. Muskrat took the stick and before long he was upright and walking.

Tiny Beaver shouted, "Stop, Little Hawk! I have something for you!"

He lifted some old bark on top of a stump that had

been hollowed out and reached inside. He handed Little Hawk a pouch. Not just any pouch, but the same one his father had made him.

Little Hawk was amazed to see all of his possessions. Necklaces, beads, bracelets and clothing...they were all there.

"These belong to you Little Hawk," Tiny Beaver said.

The boys gathered all the materials and clothing and headed back to the cave.

After sprucing up, Little Hawk showed the boys the proper way to make a fire. Before long it was blazing. Each boy was given the tools necessary to start a fire. At first, they failed to even get the wood to smolder. Little Hawk was patient with them. The voice at which he used to instruct the boys was calm and low pitched.

"Hold pressure downward when spinning the stick in your hand. That pressure will cause the wood to become hot, hot enough to become a small ember. Try again. You'll get it," Little Hawk said.

After a few failed attempts, Running Bear saw smoke rise from the wood. He took material from the forest floor and dumped the ember in the middle. Gently he blew, and smoke poured out from his hands. Again, he blew, resulting in even more smoke appearing. One final breath and flames shot from the cluster of leaves and fine twigs Running Bear held in his hands. The three boys began to whoop and cheer as the fire burned bright. Tiny Beaver and Muskrat each took their turns. They too were able to start a fire. The boys were very pleased with their accomplishments, none more so than Little Hawk. He had taken the knowledge that was given to him and passed it on to the others. He sat back and watched quietly as they congratulated one another.

With each passing day, Running Bear was gaining strength in his leg. He could stand and take a few steps. Muskrat was able to walk without his crutch, but still limped, as his ankle wasn't fully healed.

Nights were most difficult for Little Hawk. He had trouble falling asleep. When only the crackling of the fire could be heard, his mind wondered. He would stare at the boys who had filled his life with fear. Even though he was proud of himself for taking them in, questions swirled in his head. Have I done the right thing? Will they regain their strength and attack me once again? As he could think no more, his eyes became heavy and he fell asleep.

In the morning, the cave was empty. The boys were gone. Little Hawk thought the worst. "I knew it!" he shouted aloud. "Why am I so foolish?"

As the worst of thoughts swirled through his brain, Little Hawk caught movement in the thick brush. It was Tiny Beaver. Little Hawk hid behind a large tree. He wanted to attack Tiny Beaver before he could be attacked. He slid his knife from its sheath. It glistened in the dappled sunlight through the trees.

Little Hawk noticed that Tiny Beaver was carrying a load of wood in his arms. Hiding the knife behind his back, Little Hawk stepped out from behind the tree.

"Where do you want me to stack this wood Little Hawk?" asked Tiny Beaver. At first, Little Hawk didn't reply. He couldn't. He was too shocked and ashamed to answer.

"Place it near the back of the cave. It will stay dry there," Little Hawk finally answered. After Tiny Beaver had passed, Little Hawk slipped his knife back into its place.

While answering Tiny Beaver's question, Little Hawk looked up and noticed the other boys walking from the same direction and both carrying a load of wood. Running Bear was carrying what he could in spite of the terrible limp.

"I hope this will be enough to get us through the next few days," said Running Bear. "Looks like a storm is on the horizon."

With enough wood for a week stockpiled in the cave and more than enough meat prepared, the boys spent the coming days inside. At first there was an uncomfortable silence. No one spoke. Then Running Bear began to scold his friends.

"I can't believe I was left alone to be killed by the bear! Cowards!" Running Bear shouted. "How could you leave me at a time like that?" He wanted an answer, but none was given. The two others just stared at the ground in shame.

"If it wasn't for Little Hawk being as brave as he is, I'd be dead!" Running Bear turned toward Little Hawk.

"Where did you find the courage?" he asked.

"I had seen the attack before in a dream. I knew one day I would face the greatest of beasts." He paused. "I didn't know where or when it would happen, or that confronting it would save your life, but I knew I would face it one day." His answer was clear to Running Bear. He now knew that Little Hawk was the bravest person he had ever known. His respect for him was immense.

Running Bear turned his attention back to Tiny Beaver and Muskrat. "The two of you put together don't have half the courage and bravery of Little Hawk!"

"Where did you learn how to do all this?" asked Tiny Beaver, pointing to everything in the cave. He wanted to change the subject, as he felt ashamed of his behavior. But before Little Hawk could answer, he asked another question. "How can you remember it all?"

"My family taught me all I would need to know," Little Hawk replied. "If you like, I can teach you as I was taught. If so, you must do exactly as you are told."

"Like with the fire," Running Bear said. The three boys all nodded their heads in approval.

"Let us rest," said Little Hawk. "We have been

through a lot and there is so much to learn." They all lay down and fell asleep, all but Little Hawk. After a few minutes, he sat up and stared at the boys as they slept. Little Hawk smiled and thought of the days ahead. He couldn't believe that the boys who once tormented him were now going to be his students. A feeling of relief came over him. A sense of belonging that he had never felt before made him smile. And for the first time in a long time, he went to sleep free from fear.

# 17

The next day, Little Hawk had each of the boys work on arrowheads. He started with the best places to find the stones. He took them down to the stream and pointed to a bend along the creek. They quickly picked stones to work on.

After they chose the stones, Little Hawk showed his new allies how to transform a simple stone into a razor sharp, bone-breaking masterpiece. He presented each lesson only one time to all three boys. And they learned quickly. Little Hawk was astonished at how fast they picked up and retained the information.

Sometimes Tiny Beaver and Muskrat would have difficulty. So, Running Bear would take the time and help them to ensure their comprehension of the lesson. Little Hawk was pleased as he could see a change in Running Bear.

Little Hawk also taught lessons dealing with food preparation for consumption as well as for storage. Meat was dried and smoked over the fire. He showed the boys where to find the best nuts and berries in the forest. Many were gathered. Little Hawk showed them how to set them out to dry in the sunlight. Running Bear snatched a nut from the group and popped it in his mouth. Little Hawk grinned. Running Bear grabbed another, but before he could consume it, Little Hawk quickly reached out and held onto Running Bear's wrist. His eyes widened. Little Hawk let go and the four boys laughed heartily.

Finally, they were taught how to spear fish. In the beginning, Little Hawk let them experience a bit of failure. They would thrust their spears into the water directly over the fish. They would catch nothing.

Little Hawk chuckled slightly and then asked them why they weren't successful. Muskrat and Tiny Beaver were clueless and couldn't figure out why this was happening. But not Running Bear. He was bright and figured out what was the problem.

"It's the water! It must make the fish look closer or farther away than they actually are," he said.

"Yes, the water makes them appear farther away, so your spear must enter the water closer to you," said Little Hawk.

Running Bear took the advice and was quickly taking fish from the stream. He turned to Little Hawk and asked, "How many fish should I take?"

Muskrat chimed in, "Only as much as you or we can eat at one time. We don't want the food to go to waste."

Even Tiny Beaver mentioned the fact that they could use a few of the fish to help their plants grow bigger and healthier. Little Hawk was impressed with what they were learning in such a short time.

The next lesson for the boys to learn involved hunting and trapping. The most important aspect of hunting was not to be heard. This was Little Hawk's favorite lesson to teach.

The boys were very loud as they walked through the forest.

"The three of you sound like a herd of buffalo stampeding through the forest," Little Hawk said.

He taught them to move like his grandfather had shown him while scanning not only the forest for game, but also the path on which they were walking.

"You must search for litter on the path. Broken twigs or branches, even large dry leaves can be very loud," Little Hawk pointed to the path.

He began to show the others just how to step, heel-to-toe. This was the quietest way to walk through the forest.

The boys were concentrating hard on the forest floor. They were so concerned with the level of noise they were making that they didn't notice that Little Hawk had slipped into the brush and was gone.

"Listen!" whispered Running Bear. "We'll hear him walking. Be quiet!" Try as they might, not a sound was heard. A crow cawing loudly overhead was the only sound breaking the silence.

Suddenly, they heard the low growl of a wolf directly behind Tiny Beaver. His eyes bulged, ready to pop from his head. He began to tremble. Then a voice whispered in his ear. "Walk quickly and quietly through the brush as if you were as light as a feather," It was Little Hawk's voice.

Tiny Beaver jumped when he heard the voice. Running Bear and Muskrat fell to the ground in laughter. At first, Tiny Beaver was embarrassed and angry, but soon he was able to see the humor and chuckled too.

After the boys had gathered themselves and got the laughter out of their systems, Little Hawk helped the others make their own bows and arrows. He also then taught them how to shoot. Within a week the three boys were excellent marksmen. One of Running Bear's arrows actually clipped the end of Muskrat's arrow, rendering it useless. They were shooting them so accurately and in such tight groups that they decided to pull each arrow directly after it was shot. Making the arrows was a tedious job, so ruining one in target practice was a waste.

The most important lessons left were of a spiritual nature. These lessons took place around the fire, after the day had all but ended. Little Hawk told them how important each individual was to the village. The tribe always came first. Everyone had his or her own job to do and it all benefitted the tribe.

The boys also learned that the spirits of their fallen brothers and sisters reentered the world in the bodies of the animals around them. And when an animal was taken, "thanks" must be given to that spirit. Little Hawk explained that when he took the rabbit, he gave thanks to the spirit of the rabbit. It would feed him now and keep him warm in the winter. The fish he took from the stream had the same importance. They would be consumed and also placed into the ground with seeds of corn and squash to help them grow.

Little Hawk passed all the knowledge onto the boys who once had tormented him. He felt great satisfaction in teaching them all he knew. But worry and doubt began to surface once again. Thoughts of how they had treated him in the past kept creeping into his mind. He couldn't drive these thoughts from his head.

The next day, Little Hawk was out gathering nuts and berries when he noticed Running Bear, whose leg had now been completely healed, take his bow and head for the forest. He followed Running Bear at a distance, so he wouldn't be detected. Little Hawk watched as Running Bear stalked a small deer. He moved quickly and quietly. The deer had no idea he was there. Little Hawk was impressed.

Running Bear drew an arrow and sent it spiraling

into the deer's ribs. It bucked and kicked high into the air and staggered off into the brush.

After a few minutes, Running Bear was up and tracking the animal. Little Hawk followed. He watched as Running Bear found his prey. He approached the deer and set his bow gently on the ground beside the expired animal. He began to recite the verse that Little Hawk had taught him. He was giving thanks to the spirit. Little Hawk was amazed.

A great sense of pride now completely filled Little Hawk. He crouched behind a small bush and quietly made his way back to the cave.

Upon his return, Little Hawk said nothing to the others about Running Bear's deer. He went on about his business gathering wood. Soon Running Bear appeared with the carcass. Muskrat and Tiny Beaver immediately dropped what they were doing and took out their knives. They took the deer from Running Bear, who looked exhausted from hunting it and bringing it back by himself and began to work on the carcass. Before long, they skinned the deer, turned the hide inside out, and were ready to clean it.

The two boys worked with incredible efficiency. The entire deer was used...the hide, meat and even the bones. Nothing was wasted.

The cooperation and speed at which things were done was impressive. Running Bear looked up and asked about the crops growing next to the cave. Little Hawk walked to the corn, insisting that the three boys follow him. He grabbed an ear of corn and pulled a bit of the husk off, revealing the kernels inside and told Running Bear to take a small bite of the ear. The kernels popped with sweet juice to the delight of Running Bear. Little Hawk told them that if the kernels are hard and bitter tasting, they are not ready.

"These burst in my mouth and are sweet tasting. They are ready to be picked," Running Bear said.

Little Hawk told the boys how many to harvest for that day. He watched as they picked many ears and carried them into the cave. Some of the ears were wrapped and placed near the fire to be cooked. Most were set aside so the kernels could dry out. Once all moisture was stripped from the ears, they would be shucked. Finally, the individual kernels of corn would be ground into powder and used to make cornbread. Little Hawk was very impressed at what he witnessed this day. He could now put all doubt and fear he felt behind him. The anxiety of interacting with these boys was now laid to rest.

# 18

As the leaves on the trees had fallen and were scattered on the forest floor, the boys began to talk about the quickly approaching winter. The first thoughts of separating began to surface. There was an uncomfortable silence when the boys sat to eat. They knew what they should do, but no one wanted to actually say it. Little Hawk then began to speak of the importance of asking their ancestors for advice by looking into the world of the spirits. He told of the ancestors helping him make the decision to return to the tribe to get the medicine to save Running Bear's life.

The boys decided that Little Hawk would make the drink to help the others look into the spirit world. Little Hawk was nervous, however, that their ancestors would be upset that they were breaking the rules to the Seasons Away. He made the drink and served a portion to each of the boys. They gulped it down and waited to be transported to the world of the spirits.

Just as before, a thick fog rolled into the cave.

Muskrat and the others were frightened. Little Hawk stood and walked into the mist. The others followed. They all went into the spirit world together, single file. They passed several old women who smiled at the boys and looked pleased. One woman sent them each in different directions. They went their separate ways.

Muskrat and Tiny Beaver witnessed many women cleaning the hide of a buffalo. When the job of cleaning the buffalo hide was complete, the women smiled at each other and went in their own direction. Everyone seemed to be going on their own once their tasks were finished.

Running Bear's experience was not as pleasant. As he walked through the fog and into the spirit world, several people shuffled about in front of him. One man turned and looked directly at him. Running Bear could only see the man's left shoulder and head as he seemed to disappear in the crowd. He ran toward this man. Others looked at him in disgust. He walked on. It happened again. Running Bear saw a tall man with long black hair standing in the crowd, shaking his head in disappointment. Three women strolled past, catching his attention for a split second. He stepped past them and ran in the man's direction. "Father!" Running Bear called out in desperation. His scream was in vain as the man once again disappeared. Running Bear felt his heart sink. He was sure it was his father. He is disappointed in me, he thought. I must change my ways.

Little Hawk walked through the crowd of people. He could tell by the looks and nods that they approved of his actions. He smiled eagerly and nodded back, acknowledging their approval. The fog was back, waiting to return him. He slowly walked into the mist and before he knew it, he was next to the fire. Each of the boys found themselves sick to their stomachs. After a quick drink of water, they recovered and talked about what they saw.

Tiny Beaver was the first to speak and clearly understood what everything meant. He said that they were not to stay together any longer.

"Our ancestors were pleased that we have come together and mended our differences. But we must not stay together," he continued. "The purpose of our Seasons Away is for each of us to find ourselves, to depend on the knowledge that was given to us. We must do it alone."

The others agreed. Tiny Beaver continued, "Little Hawk, you have been kind when we have not. Without you, we would not be here and have an opportunity to complete this challenge. I won't stay here and increase your chances of being thrown out of the tribe. When the sun rises, I will leave."

"Running Bear, you are very quiet. Are you okay?" Little Hawk asked.

"I saw someone in the spirit world," Running Bear replied quietly.

"Who?" the others asked simultaneously.

"My father," Running Bear replied. Tiny Beaver and Muskrat were pleased that Running Bear was able to see his father again.

"Did he speak to you?" Little Hawk asked.

"No," he said in the most sorrowful voice the boys had ever heard. "He looked so disappointed in me. Every time I tried to get close, he'd walk away and fade into the crowd."

The others knew this wasn't good and an eerie silence filled the cave. Running Bear stood ready to leave when Little Hawk spoke.

"Let us enjoy this last meal together," Little Hawk insisted. "One last fire." He wanted to change the subject as he could tell that this encounter made Running Bear very sad.

The boys were awake long into the night telling stories and talking about the coming winter. Anything to occupy Running Bear's mind and keep him from thinking of his father. A tremendous feeling came over Little Hawk, a feeling of belonging, a sense of brotherhood so strong that it paralleled the love and compassion he felt for his own family. He didn't want this night to end.

Little Hawk pulled out the necklace he made from

the enormous bear claws. Running Bear's eyes widened as the attack flashed in his mind. Little Hawk untied the back of the necklace and removed three of the huge claws. He handed each of the boys a piece of thinly sliced rawhide.

Muskrat jokingly said, "What a great gift Little Hawk! How can we ever repay you?" The boys chuckled and then all was quiet.

Little Hawk handed each of them one of the claws from his necklace. "When you are in a place of great confusion, rub this claw and remember our time together," Little Hawk said.

There was a long pause and then he continued. "I have given it much thought and I realize that we are as close as brothers. I think about what has happened between us and know now that won't happen again. I must tell you, all I ever wanted was your friendship. That is what I have desired."

The others were ashamed to look at Little Hawk as they knew what they had done was wrong. They each put the necklace containing the one bear claw around their necks. "We are sorry for the way we treated you, Little Hawk. You have saved us and for that one day the favor will be repaid," answered Running Bear.

After handing the boys their necklaces, Little Hawk presented three beautiful feathers from a red-tailed hawk that he had taken with his bow. He handed one feather to each of the boys. Tiny Beaver and Muskrat chose to use the feather to make a dream catcher. Running Bear weaved the feather into his hair. It dangled from the side of his head, making him look older, like one of the men of the village. Without a word, Running Bear stared Little Hawk in the eye. He nodded, not only accepting the gift, but also acknowledging the depth of friendship that such a gift carries. With the light of the fire growing dim, the boys lay down. The cave echoed with the sounds of humming and singing, reminding Little Hawk of the sounds of the village. The songs calmed all three boys.

When the sunlight came through the entrance of the cave, warming Little Hawk's face, he sat up and noticed the boys had already gone. Left just outside the cave was a note, a collection of pictures scribbled on a piece of beech bark. The pictures consisted of a crude sketch of the bear attack, the four boys together around a fire and a tall, proud looking brave holding a bow and arrow. At the bottom was a picture of four figures standing side by side. The last was of a face with three huge scars across it. Little Hawk knew right away that Running Bear had left this behind. He picked up the note revealing the necklace that lay underneath. It was the necklace his mother had made. Running Bear had snatched it from his neck just before the Seasons Away. Little Hawk clutched the necklace tightly in his hand and longed to speak to his friends again.

With the boys together for months, the cave had been full of stories, laughter and life. But now, as it was on the first day, the cave had fallen silent. A deafening quiet gripped Little Hawk and settled into his chest. The hole through the middle of Little Hawk that had been filled with camaraderie and brotherhood for the past few weeks was now gapingly wide. He felt terribly alone again.

# 19

When the snow began to fall and continued throughout the long, cold winter, Little Hawk worried about his new friends. He hoped he had taught them enough to make it through. He tried to put those negative thoughts out of his mind and focus on the tasks at hand. But it was hard. Little Hawk thought of them often. He occupied his mind by setting a few traps. He caught a few rabbits and worked on their hides.

He walked to the wall of the cave that had several pictures drawn on them. He began to draw his own pictures. He drew a picture of the bear attack. Little Hawk even drew pictures of the boys sitting together making the decision to leave and fulfill their own destinies by completing the Seasons Away on their own. Drawing not only helped Little Hawk pass the time but also helped him to remember the good times he had with his newly found friends.

One evening Little Hawk stood at the entrance of the cave and watched the sun set along the horizon. A deep, dark cherry red color gave way to an almost blueish purple haze. A magnificent sight to behold. He knew that this night was going to be cold, the coldest of the year so far. There were no clouds in the sky to hold the heat of the earth. As the beautiful red/blue sky gave way to a sky dappled with twinkling stars, Little Hawk took a deep breath inward through his nose. The fresh cold air had frozen the hair in his nostrils and tickled the back of his throat. He coughed slightly and realized that he must prepare for this onslaught of bitterly cold air that had descended upon him.

Before he was ready to lie down for the night, Little Hawk had stoked the fire and placed several flat stones on the edge of the fire ring. While the fire burned strong, he began to dig a very shallow oval shape in the dirt floor where he slept. Then he lined the oval-shaped bowl with pine pitch to soften the bottom. Next, Little Hawk quickly grabbed the hot stones and placed them on the pine pitch until the entire oval shaped bowl looked like the inside of a turtle shell. He placed more pine pitch over the hot stones and then they were covered with the blanket of a deer hide. Finally, Little Hawk himself laid on the deer hide and pulled a very thick and heavy buffalo hide over his body.

The heat from the stones would radiate up through the pine pitch, through the deer hide and be trapped by his body and the buffalo blanket pulled over him. By doing this, Little Hawk kept himself warm during the brutally cold night. He would use this technique several more times during periods of bitter cold that seemed relentless and unforgiving. Little Hawk thought himself clever and chuckled at his own brilliance and ability to stay warm. However, he wasn't so sure his friends were as clever.

Little Hawk sat by the fire under many skins during a long cold spell, which had dumped several inches of snow over many days. He became concerned with Running Bear's wellbeing. He thought about the rules of the Seasons Away and realized that there was no rule that would exclude him from taking him food and supplies without Running Bear's knowledge. This way nobody, except Little Hawk (and perhaps the ancestors), would know he was helping his brother.

He packed some supplies and trail mix, which consisted of nuts and dried berries, then began his search for Running Bear. Little Hawk needed to know he was okay. The snow was falling so quickly that he could barely see his own tracks. The evergreen trees had collected so much snow that their branches were nearly brushing the ground. Little Hawk sought refuge from the squall under one of the low hanging branches. He covered himself with a skin and took out a small pinch of trail mix and began to nibble. In a short while the snow let up and he resumed his search. As he approached a ridge, he caught a faint whiff of smoke in the air. He cautiously maneuvered to a spot where he could observe without being seen. He was unsure who was living in this area.

Before long a thin young man emerged from the small dwelling. He looked to be weak. He stretched his arms and turned so that Little Hawk could see his face. His face was thin and drawn, but it was Running Bear, no doubt.

Little Hawk at first wanted to shout and wave in his direction. But before he let his emotions get the better of him, Little Hawk stepped back and remained quiet. He would have to be clever to be able to slip into Running Bear's tent, place food and clothing inside and leave again without being detected. He watched as Running Bear left the area in search of food. Little Hawk quickly made his way into the dwelling and left several pieces of jerky, some dried berries and a pair of his warmest moccasins. He also left a huge blanket made from two deer he had taken.

He returned to his own humble abode only to realize that now that he had helped Running Bear, he felt obligated to do the same for Tiny Beaver and Muskrat. He searched for days before finding each boy. Neither was there when Little Hawk approached, but he knew they were the only ones in this area. Little Hawk found two makeshift shelters. He went inside the dwellings and left food for them to eat, including dried meat and berries. In Little Hawk's mind, he thought he had to take care of each boy, as well as himself.

There just wasn't enough time for them to learn everything! he thought. How did I get into this mess?

Now Little Hawk was hunting, gathering and making food for four people instead of just one. Many nights he went without eating because he had given his own rations of food to the others.

Little did he realize this couldn't be further from the truth. Running Bear had returned from a successful hunting trip. He cleaned and smoked the meat over his fire. He stretched the hide to dry. Running Bear then gathered all the berries and nuts that he had stored and when combined with the amount someone had brought him, his pouches were overflowing. After a week, Running Bear made his way back to Little Hawk's cave. Just before entering, he heard a small rustling sound, some sort of movement. Running Bear crept to the entrance and peered inside. He saw Little Hawk asleep by the fire. Then he heard whispering. He made his way inside only to find Muskrat and Tiny Beaver.

"What are you doing here?" Running Bear asked.

"We could ask you the same," Muskrat whispered.

"We each thought Little Hawk was bringing us food and clothing," Tiny Beaver said.

"He did the same for me!" exclaimed Running Bear quietly.

"Let's assure him we will be fine," Muskrat said.

Running Bear left dried meat and a pouch overflowing with nuts and dried berries. Muskrat and Tiny Beaver gathered wood and stoked the fire until the flames reflected high off the cave walls.

After scrambling for a week to provide food and clothing for the others, Little Hawk had realized he could do no more and collapsed by his fire. He slept for more hours now than in the previous weeks. He woke to find his own fire roaring, the meat stash well stocked and his large pouch of mixed dried fruits and berries overflowing. He couldn't believe his surroundings. Little Hawk immediately knew his friends were capable of surviving the harsh winter on their own.

Many moons were spent under heavy blankets, close to the fire deep inside the cave. Finally, he began to notice small breaks in the weather. Snow, which had been a bright and fluffy white for months, had turned a darker color, almost the color of a ripened blueberry. It was becoming heavy and beginning to melt. The days were getting longer. Spring was on its way. Concern for his friends' safety and wellbeing again dominated his thoughts. He had forgotten to tell them about the spring.

When animals emerge from their long slumber, they are very hungry. He feared the boys would be hunted more vigorously now. Little Hawk was quite nervous.

He went about his daily routine knowing he had no control over what happened to them. He could only hope they would survive.

# 20

Little Hawk counted more than 350 marks on the wall of the cave. He knew that the day to return to the village was rapidly approaching. He was extremely excited to see his family. He wanted to show his mother the new clothes he had made. He wanted to show his uncle and father the necklace and tell them about killing the bear.

Little Hawk wanted to tell the entire village about saving Running Bear's life and taking in all three boys. But he knew he could tell them none of it. This was a direct violation of the Seasons Away. Plus, Little Hawk was too modest to boast of his accomplishments. If others were to speak of it, fine, but he would never think of himself in that way.

The final few days went slowly for Little Hawk. Both days and nights were filled with the anticipation of returning to the village. His food was abundant, and he took little time to gather enough to eat. The time passed slowly.

Little Hawk was curious as to what might happen next. He went to gather more peyote to go to the spirit world. Something was different. This time the ancestors acted as if they were ashamed of him. One wrinkled man shook his head then turned his back. This was a sure sign that he was not happy. The rest did not look as pleased as they had the last two times he had visited. Little Hawk was nervous about the near future. He returned and prepared for the trip back to the tribe.

He went to the forest and proceeded to find two long trees that had been dead for some time but weren't lying on the ground. They had fallen only partway and were supported by another tree or log already on the ground. Little Hawk chose this type of small tree because he knew it would be dry and light enough for him to drag. He needed these poles to help him take all he had made and gathered over the past year. He searched every inch of the cave but could not find the rattle. He was devastated. Where was it? He always had it with him. Where could it be? Knowing he must finish preparing to go home, he gave up and accepted that it was gone.

He placed everything in the bearskin that he used as a blanket and made his last mark on the cave wall. He then drew a picture depicting the events on the day he had slain the bear. He stood to admire his artwork. He rubbed the necklace made from the claws of the great grizzly. With a sigh and a pause, he turned and exited the cave for the last time.

Outside the cave, Little Hawk had attached the bearskin blanket to the two long poles he had brought back from the forest the day before. He laid them in the shape of a "V" and had the skin connected near the open end. His parents called them "skids." He then grabbed the two poles and held them at his waist with only the back ends dragging on the ground behind him. He had seen the village move with great speed and efficiency when getting ready to migrate to warmer grounds in the winter.

Little Hawk knew the way to the village like the back of his hand. He walked almost the entire day and decided to make camp for the night. He scouted the area for the right place to make camp.

He cleared a spot and started a fire within a few minutes. He spent the night looking at his journal and nibbling on a piece of jerky, for he couldn't sleep with all the excitement of seeing his family and friends. Again Muskrat, Tiny Beaver and Running Bear entered his mind. He was thrilled that in a short time, he would see them again.

When the morning light woke Little Hawk, he made sure the fire was out and then he was on his way once again. He knew around the next bend at the bottom of the next bluff would be a beautiful sight, his home. A gently rolling hill guards the village to the east and

Little Hawk could hardly contain himself as he reached the top of the hill and saw the village below.

He walked quickly down the hill and into the tall grass leading to the village. Every ounce of his being wanted to scream at the top of his lungs and run to his mother and father. But he was different now. As much as he wanted to, he didn't. He let go of the skid he was dragging and walked calmly and confidently into the village.

Little Hawk's mother was outside the teepee taking care of a hide when she saw a young man with an unfamiliar face walking directly at her. She became alarmed. Just as she was ready to scream for help, he called to her, "Mother!" She turned but didn't know this voice. It was a deep and forceful voice. He walked closer and still she didn't recognize his face. He smiled at his mother and then she began to see.

"Little Hawk?" his mother said very puzzled. "Is that you?"

"It is," the low voice said.

She ran to her son, throwing her arms around him. She stepped back quickly, noticing that he felt uncomfortable with the embrace.

"Let me look at you!" she said. "You've grown! You are my little boy no longer, you are a man! Come, I'll take you to your father. He will be most excited to see you."

Little Hawk walked with his mother as other

members of the tribe looked on with amazement. None of them recognized Little Hawk. He walked with such confidence, head held high and broad shoulders back.

He had grown almost six inches in the past year. His features were more distinct, and his hair was long and jet-black. The most curious item about Little Hawk to the villagers was the incredible necklace he carried around his neck. The claws were enormous and the necklace itself was grand.

Many of the village members also noticed his swagger. His whole appearance was one of strength. As he walked by, he overheard an old woman mumble to herself, "The Seasons Away was very good to him."

Rolling Thunder was gathering his things for the upcoming hunt. He glanced up and knew right away his son had returned. He could barely hold back the smile as he greeted his son, now a man, for the first time. Rolling Thunder couldn't believe that he was staring almost eye-to-eye with his son.

Little Hawk saw again the look of pride on the face of his father. Neither Little Hawk nor Rolling Thunder could hold back their smiles any longer. With the family gathering around them, Rolling Thunder and Little Hawk threw their arms around one another in a long embrace.

"It's good to see you, Little Hawk," his father whispered in his ear.

"You too, Father. You too," he replied.

Little Hawk spent the rest of the afternoon walking around the village talking with the other members. Still there was no sign of his friends, with no mention of them at all. He was concerned. Little Hawk asked his father if he had seen or heard of their return. He had not.

"I'm surprised you are interested in them. I know they've given you trouble in the past. Why the sudden interest?" asked Rolling Thunder.

"I have a confession to make, Father," said Little Hawk, bowing his head in shame. Then he told him the entire story. He told them how they had attacked him and assaulted him before and during the Seasons Away. He told him about the horrible grizzly attack. Then he paused.

"Go on," his father insisted.

"I stopped the bleeding and brought him back to where I was staying. I didn't know what to do! He had been so mean and hateful toward me, yet I knew if I did nothing he would die."

Little Hawk continued. "I looked to the world of the spirits for direction. From that, I knew that I had to save him. They told me he was my brother and I must save his life."

He went on about taking in all three boys and teaching them the way of their people. "It was very satisfying, passing the knowledge onto them. I know it was wrong and I broke the rules, but they were not prepared for the trip. I hope they return and you too will see a change in them, as I have. "

Little Hawk conveniently left out the part about secretly returning to the tribe to obtain medicine. He did not want to bring shame to his family, as he knew his father would be upset.

Knowing that the rules had been broken, Rolling Thunder still couldn't help but feel a sense of pride overtake his body. His son was a better person than he.

"I may not have helped them, Little Hawk. Not because of the rules, but because of the way they treated you," his father said. "You are a better person than I. It will all be settled at the ceremony. We are off on a hunt to prepare for the great feast. Stay here and wait for your friends' return."

His father went back to gathering his things and then slipped off with the rest of the hunting party in search of buffalo. Little Hawk wanted to join them but knew he should wait for his friends.

Exhausted, Little Hawk laid down inside the teepee and fell quickly asleep. In the morning he woke to the sound of voices and laughter outside his tent. He couldn't even remember his head hitting the fur before he was asleep.

He emerged from his teepee and there stood a large

mob of people standing around Running Bear. They were all curious about the huge scars on his face. Little Hawk watched from a short distance as Running Bear told the story of the attack. He told them of a courageous warrior saving him and mending his wounds.

When asked who saved him, Running Bear said, "I had seen him before, but didn't recognize him." Running Bear answered all the questions the young boys asked. They couldn't stop staring at his scared face, but he wasn't embarrassed. He reached up and ran his fingers down each of the enormous scars. He told the children, "I am forced to wear these scars. They are a constant reminder of who I used to be." He paused, "And who I am now." One of the boys reached up and softly did as Running Bear had, running his fingers across the scars. "Wow!" was his only response.

Running Bear's mother, Ptaysanwee, watched him closely and was intrigued by his patience with the little ones and his response to them. Running Bear's leg was all but healed, but he still walked with a noticeable limp. When she realized he was walking in her direction, she quickly turned and started away.

"Mother, stop!" Running Bear called to her. Ptaysanwee did as he asked, but she did not turn to face him. He stepped in front of his mother and put his hands on her shoulders. "Please, let us talk."

The two walked the perimeter of the village while

Running Bear poured his heart out to her. "I am sorry for the pain I have caused you all these years. Nothing I can do will change what was done in the past. I can only prove to you that the future will be much different."

His mother stopped and looked at her son. She tilted her head slightly and then smiled broadly and proudly. She reached up with both her hands and touched his cheeks. She held his face and tenderly whispered, "There you are!" Running Bear was puzzled.

"The light that sparkled in your eyes when you were a little boy. It has returned."

Running Bear threw his arms around his mother and squeezed with all his might. At first, his mother didn't react. Slowly she put her arms around his back and softly kissed his cheek. As they began their walk back to their teepee, Running Bear's mother slipped her left arm inside his right and clasped her hands. She rested her head on his shoulder and continued to smile. Others sitting around the village took notice of the embrace and smiled in approval.

The two walked past Aahana and her mother. She couldn't help but stare. Running Bear smiled in her direction. She didn't return the smile. Her eyes closed with a scornful look as she knew what he had done to her younger brother.

The ceremony was set for the following evening. Everyone in the tribe would turn out for the event. The boys would be brought out to give an example of how they had grown during their time away from the tribe.

Little Hawk thought long and hard, but kept coming back to the same story, the grizzly bear. He knew he couldn't tell that story. So, he would tell of learning how fierce and unforgiving the wilderness could be if one wasn't prepared.

He still hadn't talked to any of his friends since their return. He had no idea what they might say. He wanted to talk to them. But the boys were never given the opportunity to speak to each other. The time passed slowly as the night of the ceremony took forever to arrive. Little Hawk couldn't wait for the ceremony and a chance to talk to Running Bear and the others.

# 21

The murmur of the crowd could be heard outside the chief's tent on the night of the celebration. Little Hawk, Running Bear, Muskrat and Tiny Beaver all sat quietly inside. Running Bear broke their silence. "It is good to see you again Little Hawk," he said. "You have grown!"

"I'm glad to see you too. All of you!" replied Little Hawk.

"We learned so much from you. You taught us very well," said Tiny Beaver.

The flap of the teepee opened and Chief Strong Bow stepped inside. The boys were quiet again. "Are you all ready?" he asked.

The four boys nodded and stood and faced their chief. He was holding something in his hand covered by a small piece of cloth. This was very unusual because the chief had never carried anything to the ceremony before.

They were all nervous. Tiny Beaver looked ill, with the look of someone who was about to faint.

"I have never spoken in front of this many people before! What if I blank and can't remember what to say?" he said. His voice cracked and sounded frightened. The Chief stood and with a motion of his arm, the boys stood as well.

The crowd was now silent, as they emerged from the teepee and were standing before the entire village.

"Thank you for coming. This is a glorious night for our tribe. The boys you see before you have completed their trials. Three of these boys have become men worthy of acceptance from the tribe. Men of character, honor and courage."

The crowd began to whisper. What could the chief mean? All four boys made it through the Seasons Away successfully. Why did he only mention three of them? Questions could be heard among the crowd. Even the boys were confused. All but Little Hawk. He knew right away that he had done wrong. He had broken the rules when he returned to the tribe. His heart sank.

The chief pulled the rattle from under the piece of cloth. There was a gasp from the crowd and then complete silence.

"One of these boys returned to the village. And in doing so broke the most sacred rule we have. Now he must leave us. Step forward and present yourself to the village."

The three boys looked at each other, then to Little

Hawk. His head was down, and his eyes closed as he stepped forward to accept his punishment. Not only had he shamed himself but his family as well. His heart felt like it was in the pit of his stomach.

With his head down, not wanting to see the look on his father's face, Little Hawk slowly made his way through the crowd on his way back to his teepee. Running Bear began to fidget as he watched his friend exiting the ceremony. He wanted to tell the chief the truth. That Little Hawk saved his life, taught him and the others how to survive and transformed him into the man he now is. He wanted to shout to the entire tribe why Little Hawk had returned. But he said nothing. He couldn't bring himself to tell the chief. Sweat dripped from his forehead as he could feel the stares of Tiny Beaver and Muskrat. The stares weighed heavily on his mind. It felt as if the two boys were standing on his chest. He couldn't breathe. And still he kept quiet.

Little Hawk knew that he had made a mistake. He also knew that he had to face the consequences for his actions. He passed his mother and sister but couldn't look at them. He glanced up slightly. His grandfather stood emotionless. His face had no expression. Rolling Thunder followed Little Hawk into his teepee.

"Father, I am sorry I have brought shame to you and our family," Little Hawk said in a low voice and with his back turned.

"I cannot go against the wishes of the chief, Little Hawk. You know that. I can't understand why you would risk being thrown out of the tribe in order to save someone like Running Bear," said his father.

"I had to. He is my brother. I looked to the spirits for guidance and this is the path that had been chosen for me. I knew what I had to do."

Little Hawk gathered his things and left the village that night. He was sad for many reasons. He could not shake the image of that stone cold look on his grandfather's face. Again, he felt ashamed. All the knowledge passed onto Little Hawk, now wasted.

Rolling Thunder went straight for Running Bear's teepee. He ripped the flap open and barged inside. Running Bear was waiting for him. Rolling Thunder was furious.

"This is your fault!" he barked at Running Bear.

"It is all my fault," Running Bear replied in shame. This admission of guilt caught Rolling Thunder off guard.

"Why? What did my son ever do to you to deserve such treatment?"

"Nothing," Running Bear replied.

This answer angered Rolling Thunder. He shoved Running Bear to the ground. There was no resistance.

"I deserve whatever you do to me, Rolling Thunder," Running Bear said. "In fact, I would almost welcome it at this point. My stomach is in knots and my mind won't let me rest!"

Standing over Running Bear, fists clinched, eyes as dark as the night sky, Rolling Thunder let out a long breath. Without a word, he turned and walked out of the teepee.

# 22

For several days Little Hawk stayed inside the cave that he spent the last year living in. He didn't come out; neither did he eat. He was too ashamed to function. But slowly he made some progress and began to regain his wits. He returned to the stream to catch fish. He set new traps. All the while, he thought that if Running Bear had just spoken at the ceremony maybe he wouldn't have been ousted from the tribe.

"That is selfish talk!" he said aloud. "Do not blame anyone but yourself." Little Hawk was tending his regular trapline when he caught a glimpse of someone sneaking through the saplings on the edge of the forest. He moved quickly through the brush and was ahead of the person, ready to strike if he needed to. Suddenly he realized that the person walking through the forest was Aahana.

Little Hawk was shocked to see her. He didn't want to speak. Aahana needed answers, however. She wanted to know why he would take such a risk on his tormentor.

"Poison flows from his mouth. He lies. He steals. He is not worthy of our tribe! Why Little Hawk?" she pleaded with him.

"You would not understand," Little Hawk said. "It is, what we as a people, do. We take care of each other."

"But those boys have been so mean to you! I have seen it with my own eyes!" his sister shouted.

"They are different. Talk with them and you will see. They are good men," Little Hawk calmly spoke. "Please go," he insisted. "I will not risk you getting in trouble, too."

Aahana hugged her brother and held him tightly for quite some time. She turned quickly, not wanting her brother to see her cry. Little Hawk's eyes welled with tears as he watched his sister disappear into the forest.

His thoughts turned to what his friends were doing back in the village. Going on hunts and defending the tribe from rogue bands. These were things that he always dreamed he would one day do.

But in fact, Running Bear was in a state of turmoil. He couldn't sleep. He was in a constant fog. At night he would doze off for a few minutes, then see Little Hawk alone and defenseless. He would sit up breathing heavily and covered with sweat. After several nights of not sleeping, Running Bear spoke to Tiny Beaver and Muskrat.

"What's wrong with you Running Bear?" they asked.

"You look terrible!"

"I can't sleep, I can't eat. Every thought in my head is of Little Hawk. Night after night I sit up covered in a cold sweat!" He turned away from the two boys.

Running Bear then continued. "It's not right that we are here, and he is out there all alone. If it wasn't for him, I would surely be dead and you two would have eventually met the same fate."

"What can we do about it?" asked Tiny Beaver. "The chief has spoken."

"I must go to Chief Strong Bow and tell him the truth," said Running Bear firmly.

"You mustn't! We could be thrown out as well!" shouted Muskrat.

"Still thinking of yourself, Muskrat. You obviously haven't learned a thing from Little Hawk," Running Bear said disappointedly. "The only reason we are here is because he risked everything to save us. We must tell the chief, we owe Little Hawk that much. He is our brother and our friend. And if Chief Strong Bow decides that our fate is that of Little Hawk's, then I can live with that. I cannot face another night knowing that we benefit from belonging to the tribe when we have acted in a manner that is shameful. We do not deserve to stay here," Running Bear ended his statement in a low sorrowful voice.

The others could no longer argue and knew what

needed to be done.

"You're right. We must tell the truth," Tiny Beaver said earnestly. The boys nodded in agreement.

"I will go the Chief Strong Bow in the morning," said Running Bear. "I got everyone into this mess. Maybe he will only punish me."

The three agreed, parted and went their separate ways. Instead of heading for his teepee for the night, Running Bear walked slowly with his head down to the teepee of Rolling Thunder. He stood on the outside and nervously called to both of Little Hawk's parents. Rolling Thunder stepped out.

"Be gone!" he insisted. "You have no business here!" Upon hearing the stern voice, Netis came out. She softly put her hand on her husband's shoulder. "What do you want Running Bear?" she asked quietly.

Still staring at the ground beneath his feet, Running Bear began to speak. "I came here to apologize to you, Little Hawk's parents, for I am the cause of his pain and his being banned from the tribe." Nervous, Running Bear paused to catch his breath and think of the next thing to say.

"Go on," Netis could tell he had more to say.

"Little Hawk rescued me," Running Bear said. "He saved my life."

Rolling Thunder interrupted him. "I would not have saved you!" he shouted.

"I understand. I would not have saved me either. All I know is that I am a changed person. That is a direct result of your son's efforts. He is my friend and I never thought I would say such a thing. He is the bravest and most courageous person I know."

A long and uncomfortable silence left Running Bear at a loss. "I cannot change the past or the things I did before" he said. "I can only tell you that without your son, I would not be here. I wanted you to know my feelings. I came to ask your forgiveness. Whether I get it or not is up to you." Very slowly he turned and walked away.

Aahana heard the entire conversation from inside the teepee. Pulling back the flap, she watched as Running Bear pleaded his case. Little Hawk is right, she thought. Running Bear would have never have come and confessed to Rolling Thunder if he hadn't changed his ways. She slipped out of the teepee undetected and went in search of Running Bear.

Still angry from the conversation, Rolling Thunder stormed off. Netis took a deep breath and turned to go inside. She heard a soft voice call to her. It was Ptaysanwee.

"May I have a minute of your time?" she asked. "It is very hard for me to come to you. My son was not always someone who I could be proud of." The two mothers talked for some time. Ptaysanwee concluded by saying,

"Running Bear's heart was clouded by anger. After losing his father, he tried to fill the empty hole in his heart by making others feel the way he felt. But now his mind is clear and his heart open. He has come to me. I have seen it in his eyes. I have you to thank."

"Running Bear has my son to thank," Netis said.

"That is true," Ptaysanwee said. "I hope there is a way this can be resolved so that both boys can be a part of the village again."

Netis nodded and hoped with all her heart that something could be done, as this had never happened before in the village.

That night Running Bear couldn't sleep. He kept thinking of a way to present this situation to Chief Strong Bow. Confused, he thought a walk might help him clear his head and think of the best way to talk to the chief. Looking down, Running Bear rounded the side of the teepee and walked directly into Aahana.

"Tell me about my brother," she demanded. "Tell me about the Seasons Away."

"Little Hawk is smart and brave. He killed the bear. He saved my life." Running Bear went on to tell Aahana just how things went during the time alone in the wilderness. He told her of the stories at night around the fire. He explained in detail how Little Hawk taught them everything. "It isn't right," Running Bear concluded. "It's me that should be out there, not him."

"What will happen next?" Aahana asked politely.

"In the morning, when the sun rises, I will go and tell Chief Strong Bow everything. I will accept any consequence the chief will lay upon me," Running Bear proudly responded.

Aahana reached out and gently took Running Bear by the hand. "I wish you luck when speaking to the chief."

The kindest smile that he had ever seen warmed his heart. His stomach turned a little and his cheeks became hot to the touch. Aahana softly drew her hand across the scars on Running Bear's face. "These tell the story of your transformation. You have become a man. I can see the change in you." Aahana stared deeply into his eyes. She kindly smiled and walked back to her teepee, leaving Running Bear speechless and stunned.

He returned to his teepee and went inside for the night. Awake the entire night, unable to close his eyes and rest, Running Bear stepped out of his teepee, exhausted and nervous, but knew what he had to do. Maybe after telling the truth, his conscience would finally let him rest. Running Bear approached the guard outside Chief Strong Bow's teepee and asked permission to speak to him. He was denied entry to the chief's teepee because he was already in a meeting.

"But it's urgent!" he shouted. "I need to see the chief right away!"

His persistence paid off as he was finally granted permission to enter the teepee. He opened the flap and rushed inside. He was astonished at what he saw. There in front of him sat Chief Strong Bow, Tiny Beaver and Muskrat. Running Bear's face wrinkled with confusion. Strong Bow lifted his arm and without a word invited him to sit.

"These boys have told quite a story. Is what they say the truth?" he asked.

I am ashamed of myself. Little Hawk shouldn't be the one out of the tribe. It should be me," answered Running Bear. He continued, "He taught us all the true meaning of our people, to think of others before ourselves. Now we have turned our backs on someone who represents the best of who we are."

The chief sat quietly. He was truly wise beyond his years.

"It is better to listen and think than it is to hear and react without thinking things through," Chief Strong Bow said. He gestured for the boys to leave the teepee. But before they exited the teepee Running Bear asked, "What will happen now?" Chief Strong Bow paused. "The tribe has never faced such a decision. We will gather the elders. They will decide what our next step we will be."

The boys shuffled out with Running Bear still amazed. He confronted Tiny Beaver and Muskrat.

His brow wrinkled, and eyes squinted as if closed by a brightly shining sun.

Before he could say a word, Tiny Beaver said, "Like you said, Little Hawk saved us all! We are all in this together." They nodded and walked off together to await their fate.

Running Bear heard a voice call his name. It was the sweetest sound he had heard in a long time. When he turned, Aahana waved her hand, asking him to come over.

"Did you speak to the chief?" she asked.

"I...I did," Running Bear stuttered. His stomach flipped over inside. His cheeks became flush and again were hot. He quickly glanced at her face and then back to the ground.

"You are very brave for telling him the truth. I am proud of you."

Running Bear nodded. He couldn't think of something nice to say. The silence made him uncomfortable. Aahana smiled at his awkwardness. Finally, he spoke. "The men will gather in the chief's teepee to decide what to do next. I am to wait for their decision."

Aahana darted away. Running Bear watched as she sprinted from his presence, confused as to why she had suddenly gone. Within a few minutes she returned. Running Bear smiled widely when she rejoined him. The two walked off to await word of his fate.

"Where did you go?" Running Bear asked.

"I went to ask permission to wait with you. I thought you might need some company. My father was not there, but my mother gave me permission."

"Good," was the only comment he could muster, more of a cough or a grunt than a word. He cleared his throat and kicked a pebble from the path.

The two walked to Running Bear's teepee, making small talk about the weather becoming warmer and other unimportant things. Aahana wanted to keep the conversation light. She asked several questions that she already knew the answers to but wanted to occupy Running Bear's mind while he awaited such an important decision.

Gathered in Chief Strong Bow's teepee were the wisest of the men in the tribe. One man had to be excluded. Rolling Thunder wasn't allowed to be involved. The chief knew the others would be objective when dealing with this difficult decision. He was unsure that a father would objectively make decisions about his own son's life. This was a very serious matter. Never before had anyone broken the rules to the Seasons Away.

Walking toward the chief's teepee, Rolling Thunder glanced to see two individuals sitting on the ground and enjoying a conversation. His stride slowed, and he came to a halt as he realized the two people were Aahana and Running Bear. He watched as Aahana smiled and laughed. Running Bear drew shapes in the dirt, occasionally looking up into her eyes. Something had changed. If Little Hawk, Aahana, and Netis had seen Running Bear for who he is now, maybe it was time for Rolling Thunder to accept him as well.

Suddenly, Rolling Thunder entered the teepee and the members inside immediately became quiet. "I know it is not my place to interrupt this meeting, but I would like an opportunity to speak." The chief nodded and gave his approval. He extended his arm and invited Rolling Thunder to sit. He did not. He stood and looked every man directly in the eye then began.

"Running Bear has been cruel and unkind. He has been at odds with my son for many years. That is in the past. If you speak to him now, after his experience, you will see he has changed." Rolling Thunder paused. "He is a changed person because of my son. Running Bear came to me and asked for my forgiveness. I did not give it. When I see him again, he will know he has it. I know Little Hawk broke a very sacred rule when he returned to the village. But I invite each of you to ask, would you have returned to save me, to save your own son? Look at the result of this action. Look at Running Bear." Without saying another word, he turned and left the meeting.

These were powerful words spoken by Rolling Thunder. They influenced everyone in the meeting.

After a long discussion, it was decided that a search party would be formed to find Little Hawk and bring him back before the tribe. All four boys would be given the opportunity to explain the events that had transpired during the Seasons Away. The tribe would then decide whether they could stay or if they all must leave. The chief passed the intricately carved pipe to each of the men. They placed the pipe gently to their lips, took one toke each and passed it on. This action concluded the meeting. No one was to speak of this until the boys were brought before the tribe. The chief believed that some members might have preconceived feelings about the boys and would let that influence a very important decision.

Upon leaving the meeting, Rolling Thunder intentionally walked in the direction of Running Bear and Aahana. They both jumped to their feet, feeling nervous as to what he might say. Rolling Thunder didn't speak. He looked at his daughter, then at Running Bear. He nodded. Without saying a word, he had forgiven Running Bear for the years of mistreatment. All Running Bear could do was smile and nod back.

The next morning, the men assembled and were ready to conduct a massive search for Little Hawk. As the party was leaving the village, Running Bear asked if he could join them. He thought that Little Hawk might return to the same cave that he had lived in during his time away. He could find the cave and Little Hawk quickly.

The men agreed that Running Bear could join the party. He made his way to the head of the pack and led the party to the cave.

In the meantime, Little Hawk had trapped several small animals, including a few rabbits and even a grouse. He was working on the hides of the rabbits when he heard what he thought was a familiar voice.

He looked up quickly and saw nothing. He thought he was losing his mind! "Great! Now I am hearing voices," he said aloud. "What's next? Seeing things that aren't there?"

"That's right, if those things happened that would mean you're crazy!" the voice said.

Little Hawk looked up and there at the entrance to the cave stood Running Bear. Little Hawk closed his eyes, shook his head and looked again. Running Bear, leaning against the wall, stood grinning from ear to ear. Little Hawk jumped and ran to him with a look of concern on his face.

"What are you doing here? If the tribe knows you're here, they'll throw you out as well!" He quickly looked around the outside of the cave.

"Still worried about everyone else?" Running Bear said, shaking his head back and forth. "We have come to take you back to the village."

"We?" Little Hawk asked.

As he was questioning Running Bear, the members of the search party stepped out from behind the brush.

"We...are here to take you home," remarked Running Bear.

The group helped Little Hawk gather his things once again and quickly headed in the direction of the village. They were almost there when night fell upon them. They made camp for the night. Little Hawk made the evening meal. He used the meat from the rabbits he had taken to make a stew. The members of the party sat around the fire eating and talking about the upcoming judgment.

Everyone ate except Little Hawk. He stared at the others as they ate and talked. He particularly watched Running Bear, as he did most of the talking. He was telling them how he was left to die and if it wasn't for Little Hawk, he would most definitely be dead.

As he was telling the story, he noticed that Little Hawk's eyes were locked onto him. He winked and nodded in Little Hawk's direction, acknowledging him without speaking. Then he continued.

"He saved our lives in many ways. He taught us what it means to be a TRUE member of the tribe. He transformed us and helped us to become the men we are now."

The others made comments the rest of the evening,

saying that if that story were told at the judgment, everything would be forgiven, and the four young men would be permitted to stay. Little Hawk didn't understand.

"You all will be given an opportunity to plead your case before the entire tribe. If you tell them the story that was told to us tonight, I'm sure they will understand," said Rolling Thunder. The others agreed.

"When will this take place?" asked Little Hawk.

"When we return. We will be given an opportunity to speak to the village," answered Running Bear. "If they feel we have good reasons for what was done, we can stay. If not, well…"

Morning arrived quickly and soon the party was back. The group of men walked into the village. They were greeted by many of the women of the tribe. Aahana was the first to embrace her brother. "You are right," she whispered into his ear. "They have changed. They are good men."

Little Hawk watched as she greeted her father and uncle as well. He was pleasantly surprised to see her approach Running Bear. He reached out and took both her hands inside his and smiled. The others in the party walked around the couple and proceeded to greet their wives and families.

Soon the entire tribe gathered. The chief stood as the tribe grew quiet. "These four have something to tell you. Listen to their story and their fate will be in your hands."

Tiny Beaver was the first to speak. He told a tale that was not pleasing to the members of the tribe. He spoke of selfishness and complete disregard for the rules of the tribe. Tiny Beaver talked about his indifference to the rules and how he thought they were not important for survival. Then he spoke of Little Hawk. He began by speaking of Little Hawk's intelligence and courage. Tiny Beaver ended his speech with an apology to Little Hawk. When he finished, the crowd was quiet. The boys became more nervous. They could see that many members of the tribe were not happy. Muskrat was next. When he concluded, still no one spoke. The boys began to sweat because they knew the crowd disapproved of their actions during the Seasons Away.

The third to speak was Running Bear. He stood for the longest time, silently scanning the crowd for Little Hawk's family. He began by apologizing to them for what he had done to Little Hawk. Then he continued. For the longest time, Running Bear told of the torture and ridicule they had brought onto Little Hawk. He told them of the stealing of items Little Hawk had made or been given.

He then told them of the horrific attack. He spoke of every gruesome detail. He told them about the pain, blood and blackness. He began to speak of the compassion and selflessness it must have taken for Little Hawk to put everything that had happened to him aside and not only defend Running Bear but rescue him and save his life.

"To this day it is still not clear to me why Little Hawk would risk everything... his own life, to help me." Running Bear spoke very softly. He finished by adding, "He taught us the way of our people and now we truly understand. However, if anyone is to be banished from the tribe, it should be me...NOT Little Hawk." With his head down, he thanked the tribe for the opportunity to speak and stepped back. Only Little Hawk was left. Now there was a murmur coming from the crowd. People whispered and pointed at the boys. The crowd was silent once again as Little Hawk stood to give his accounts of the Seasons Away. He took a long deep breath and was ready to speak.

Just as his mouth opened to begin, Chief Strong Bow stood and ordered him to stop. "We have heard enough. Is everything that was said tonight true, Little Hawk?"

"Yes, Chief. But I would like to add something if I could," said Little Hawk. "I wish you could have seen the way they responded to the teaching of our people. The Seasons Away is a time of change and finding one's way or purpose in life. They have done just that. We have all changed and I think it has been for the better. Before the Seasons Away, Running Bear's face was pale, and his eyes were cold and dark. Look at them now. His face tells a horrifying tale and his eyes are those of kindness, unselfishness and pride." Little Hawk paused briefly. "Our fate is in your hands. YES... I did break the rules, and I will take whatever punishment you feel is necessary. We have all done wrong. I was afraid of these three every day, but now I consider them my friends, my brothers. They are good people, men worthy of our tribe. Not having them as part of the village would be a loss."

Little Hawk's voice didn't crack, shake or lose tone. He was cool, calm and collected the entire time he spoke. Chief Strong Bow looked pleased, as did many members of the tribe.

The chief stood again to speak. "Go to my teepee and wait for me there. I will bring with me the decision of the tribe."

The four boys walked slowly to the chief's teepee and sat quietly inside. They didn't look at each other and instead stared at the ground, too nervous to speak. Then the flap opened and in stepped Chief Strong Bow.

"The tribe has spoken and so it is that the four of you will be sent out..." He paused, and the boys' hearts and hopes sank. The chief continued, "You will be sent out to face the tribe and receive your adult names."

They all looked up, their mouths agape. Then smiles as wide as their face appeared.

"Thank you, Chief!" they said simultaneously. They crawled out of the teepee and the entire tribe was waiting for them. The crowd erupted into cheers and whoops of joy. Muskrat and Tiny Beaver were swept away by the tribe members. People gathered around Little Hawk and Running Bear, pulling them in different directions. Some wanted to hear more about the attack, others wanted to hear about how Little Hawk had defeated the beast. In a brief moment, the two's eyes met. Little Hawk could not hear what Running Bear said, but he didn't have to. He read Running Bear's lips. He simply said, "Thank you."

That night, around the largest fire the village had ever seen, the boys officially received their adult names and became men of the tribe. Tiny Beaver was now known as Quick Spear, Muskrat as Soaring Eagle and Running Bear as Red Feather. There was a story behind each name and Running Bear's was no exception. During the Seasons Away, Little Hawk had taken a red-tailed hawk and presented a few tail feathers to Running Bear to decorate his own headdress. He wore them with pride.

The last of the boys stepped toward the chief. Little Hawk stood straight and true, chest out, shoulders back. He stood with pride. Little Hawk's name reflected the courage and fearlessness it took to confront the largest of all beasts, the great grizzly bear. He was now known throughout the village as Stalking Grizzly. His name and the story of the bear spread over the other plains tribes like wildfire. Later that same night, as the ceremony was ending, Red Feather finally had a chance to speak to Stalking Grizzly alone.

"You saved us once again. I don't know how I can ever repay you for what you have done for me," Red Feather said.

"Your friendship was all I ever wanted. One day, I'm sure something will happen and the favor will be repaid. Let's not worry about that right now," replied Stalking Grizzly.

That night when Red Feather laid down to rest, he had no trouble falling asleep, nor did he wake in a cold sweat. He slept guilt-free until morning.

Later that evening, after everything had calmed down and people were returning to their own teepees for the night, Stalking Grizzly finally had the chance to speak to Aahana. They walked through the village, as fires were burning low. Small flames flickered and embers glowed orange and red in the night. "I couldn't have done this without you," Stalking Grizzly admitted to his sister. "You gave me an invaluable gift."

"What gift was that?" Aahana asked curiously.

"Confidence, in myself," Stalking Grizzly replied. His older sister nodded.

"I have a gift for you." Stalking Grizzly reached around the back of his neck and untied a piece of string. Hidden under his large necklace of bear claws was a separate necklace having only one claw, just like the one he gave to Red Feather and the others.

"The courage and strength I had gained to face every challenge this year, I got from you."

Stalking Grizzly stood behind his sister and tied the necklace around the back of her neck. Aahana rubbed the enormous claw and stared at it for the longest time. She spoke no words. Her only reaction was to throw her arms around her now much taller brother and squeeze. Aahana vowed to wear the necklace every day for the rest of her life, for it was the closest she would ever get to the Seasons Away herself.

After the longest silence, Aahana finally spoke. "I have seen greatness in you, Stalking Grizzly. One day you will be a great leader."

Stalking Grizzly didn't know what to make of this statement. He was satisfied enough to be back in the village and among the people of his tribe.

Wanting to lighten the mood, Stalking Grizzly bumped his sister and asked, "What is going on with you and Red Feather?" Aahana's face became hot and her cheeks flushed. Her heart began to beat faster. "He is a new person," she replied. "I like him very much."

"Good," was all Stalking Grizzly needed to say. Aahana was pleased with his approval.

Standing outside their own dwelling, Rolling

Thunder and Netis were watching as Aahana hugged her brother. They smiled at the embrace and went inside, full of pride.

The following day there was talk in the village of the white man. They were moving west and would soon be encroaching on their lands. Many of the men wanted to stay and fight the white men off. Others wanted to flee further west to the base of the great mountains that touch the sky.

It was decided that the tribe would suffer too many casualties if it were to stay and fight. And so it was that they would move the entire village west. Chief Strong Bow made the announcement and the tribe began preparations for the move. That night the tribe had one last gathering to say goodbye to the land they called home.

"When the sun rises in the east, we will begin the journey to our new land," announced Chief Strong Bow.

After the last gathering, Stalking Grizzly spoke to his uncle and father about the upcoming move. He assured them that it was necessary for the survival of the tribe. He had seen it in a vision. Following the discussion, Stalking Grizzly fell asleep to the faint beating of the drums heard just outside his teepee. When he rose in the morning, he quickly stepped outside to join his fellow tribesmen and begin their journey west.

# 23

Stalking Grizzly raised his arms high in the air, stretching and yawning. The sun shone brightly in his eyes. He squinted and took a deep breath. He was startled when his arm was grabbed and held tightly. Quickly he jerked his arm, trying to get free. But the grip was too tight.

A man dressed in a dark blue uniform with a shiny badge and a patch on his sleeve shouted at him in a language he didn't understand.

"How did you get in there?" the man shouted.

Stalking Grizzly didn't answer. He couldn't. He was confused and still couldn't understand what this man was saying to him. The man shouted again.

"Answer me, Boy! How did you get in there? What were you doing in there?"

Stalking Grizzly looked himself over from head to toe. He was wearing tennis shoes, blue jeans and a brightly colored t-shirt. But HOW? he thought.

The security guard tugged Stalking Grizzly and

dragged him away from the teepee. "I'm taking you to the head office," he continued shouting. "They'll deal with you there!"

Stalking Grizzly desperately scanned the area for someone to help him. He shouted for Red Feather, but no one came. The guard looked at him strangely and then told him to keep quiet.

As he was being dragged away, he noticed a woman running toward them. She screamed, "Ryan! Where have you been?"

He began to understand what these people were saying. "Mom?" he asked in a soft voice.

"What is going on here? Do you know this boy, Ma'am?" the guard asked harshly.

"Yes, he is my son. We were separated, and we have been looking for him the entire day. Thank you for finding him!" his mother answered.

"He slipped inside this teepee. That is forbidden. If there is any damage, you will be responsible!" The guard stared at Ryan angrily.

With incredible confusion, Ryan walked with his family and the security guard to the main office. There he explained what happened. He told them all he did inside was sleep.

The guard inspected the teepee and the administrators agreed that Ryan had caused no damage. After a long lecture, Ryan's family was released with only a warning.

As the entire family walked back to the car, Ryan could feel the heavy stares from his sister.

"What are you looking at?" he asked her.

"You look different," she replied.

"How, different? Good or Bad?" he asked.

"GOOD!" she answered. "Better, more confident. You walk differently. You have a spring in your step that I never noticed before." That was the first compliment Shelly had ever given him.

Ryan smiled at her and she smiled back. Then he thought, What a dream! It felt so real! He shrugged it off and continued to the car with his family.

The remainder of the trip, Ryan was quiet. He thought of nothing but the dream. It still felt so real. He could remember things so vividly, as if they had actually happened. He even felt like a new person, as if the dream had an effect on him mentally.

The Rocky Mountains rose from the plains and seemed to touch the sky. He had an intense feeling of déjà vu. Although he was seeing them for the first time, something about the mountains was familiar. Ryan kept quiet and spent the time in Yellowstone National Park trying to figure out what had happened to him.

The family finished their four-day stay at Yellowstone. Even though he was very intrigued by Old Faithful and the beauty that surrounded him, Ryan couldn't shake the dream from his thoughts. They packed the car and began their long trip back across the United States.

# 24

With the vacation all but over and the Mississippi River now behind them, Ryan's focus was on home. There were only three weeks left in the school year and... OH NO! Ryan thought. Jake Farlow! His mind had been so occupied by the dream that he had completely forgotten about his problems at home.

The car pulled onto their street and Ryan's dad found a spot just in front of their building. Ryan helped his dad unload the car, as his mother and sister carried their bags inside.

"Dad," Ryan said as he pulled the last of the suitcases from the back, "have you ever had something happen to you that felt so real, but you know really didn't take place?"

"When the time is right, Ryan, we'll talk about things like this," said his father. "Take your bag and get to bed."

"But you knew, didn't you?" Ryan asked.

"What I know is that you cannot hide from who you are. Ryan, you come from a long bloodline of Lakota.

You now have the strength and confidence to do what it is that needs to be done. You are becoming a man. I know my work has taken me away from our family and, more specifically, you. Some things are changing at work. I am putting in for a promotion. I should get it. When that happens, my office will be downtown, and I will be home every night. I will only have to travel once or twice a year for conferences. I will be here to help you with anything you need."

Ryan's eyes opened widely, and he threw his arms around his father.

"Now take your things into the house and get to bed. It is very late," Ryan's father said. He watched as Ryan carried his bags into the house. A proud smile appeared on his face.

Ryan dragged himself into his room and flopped onto his bed. He was so tired that he couldn't remember his head hitting the pillow.

The morning alarm rang, and Ryan jumped to his feet. He was still wearing all his clothes and even his shoes from the night before. Quickly, he stripped and was in and out of the shower before anyone else in his family was awake. The only exception was his father. Ryan's dad was already gone. He had a big meeting at the headquarters of the company. Everyone slept so soundly that they didn't hear him get up and get ready to leave.

With his mother still sleeping, Ryan tiptoed past his parents' room to the hallway closet. He was hoping to wear a new pair of shoes he got just before they went on the trip. His parents wouldn't let him wear them on vacation for fear of getting them dirty or damaged due to all the walking they would do. The shoes were bright white with a dark blue stripe on the side. Ryan was proud to own such a pair. The shoes were still in the box on the top shelf. Ryan had to stand on another box just to reach them. As he pulled them to his chest, Ryan's foot slipped off the box on which he was standing, spilling its contents. He made such a racket, he was sure it woke his mother. Ryan waited, motionless. Nothing stirred from her room.

He knelt down to set everything right and noticed a small leather book. It had a rough sketch drawn on the cover of a stick figure holding a spear over a creek. Ryan opened the book and began to look at everything inside.

He looked closely at one of the pictures. It was of a boy shooting an arrow just above a bear's head. The arrow actually took a small piece of the bear's left ear.

Ryan couldn't believe what he was looking at. This was the same bear he had killed in his dream. It had a tear in its ear. How could his dream have the same bear in it as this journal that he found in the hallway closet?

His mother rolled over in her bed. The faint noise startled Ryan. He quickly put the journal back where he had found it.

Walking the first block to school, Ryan could think of nothing but the journal. It was just like the one he had in the dream. How would his father be in possession of such an item? Where did it come from? he asked himself. Maybe he bought it at the reservation. This calmed his thoughts as he approached the alleyway leading to the school. He needed to be focused.

A pit bull barked loudly from across the street in Allegheny Manor. A lady yelled through a screen for it to stop barking. The dog ignored its owner and continued to bark menacingly. Finally, Ryan turned his attention away from the dog and to the alley directly ahead of him.

Today was the day he would stand up to Jake. He had a newly found courage. This was something he had to do. Maybe Jake would see that he wasn't going to just take the daily abuse. Maybe he would respect Ryan for actually taking a stand. Or maybe Ryan would be pummeled into the pavement. Either way it was worth the risk. He wasn't going to take the abuse anymore!

The sun shone brightly that morning. Only the alley was still covered in a dark shadow. He thought again about the bear in his dream, how terrified he was. There was a rush of adrenaline that surged through his veins when he faced the great beast. Ryan felt that same rush as he stepped into the shadow of the alley.

He swallowed hard, took a deep breath and headed straight into the darkness. He walked past Sam and Vince and glared at them. They quickly surrounded Ryan, making any type of retreat impossible. That was okay with Ryan as he was not going to retreat today. He noticed someone leaning against the wall. He saw shoes, then legs, and finally he stepped out. It was Jake. He was wearing a baseball cap pulled down so that the bill covered his eyes. Ryan could not see his face. Something was dangling from the back of the cap. Ryan could not see exactly what it was. With his head down, Jake stood directly in front of Ryan. The only ray of sunlight lay directly on the Eagles hat that Jake wore. The time was now!

Ryan thought to go on the offensive. He would swing his book bag at Jake's face, knocking him off balance, then attack Sam and Vince. If it was a surprise attack, he might have a chance. Jake stood in the only beam of sunlight that entered the alley. Ryan could see Jake's breath in the brisk morning air.

Just as Ryan was getting ready to strike, Jake looked up in the light. Ryan dropped his book bag. His eyes nearly popped from their sockets! Jake's face was terribly scared! Three enormous scars crossed his face from his hairline over his left eye and ended just under his chin. Ryan stood motionless, his jaw almost touching the pavement under his feet. Jake grinned at Ryan.

"My friendship is all you ever wanted," he said quietly.

"Wh..." Ryan stuttered, still unable to grasp what was going on around him. "WHAT?"

"My friendship. My friendship is all you ever wanted, right?" Jake paused. "Well, you will have it from now on."

Sam and Vince showed Ryan the necklaces that they all had around their necks. Each one had a single bear claw held by a thin piece of leather.

Ryan's face wrinkled with confusion. "But HOW?" he asked.

"The Seasons Away is a time for change, a time to grow. You taught us that," Jake said.

Still in disbelief, Ryan looked around to see if this was actually happening. "We owed you everything then, and we owe you everything now," Jake said as he put his arm around Ryan's shoulder. "Come on, we're going to be late."

Jake picked up Ryan's book bag and handed it to him. The four boys walked the remaining block together. Jake began to tell Ryan a story of a bad car accident that scarred his face. As they made their way to the front doors of the school, Jake said, "At least that's what we'll tell everyone. Only we know what really happened."

The doors to the school opened and the four boys walked inside.

# 25

From that day on, Ryan didn't worry about school. He met Jake, Sammy and Vince at the candy store every morning. They talked about the summer and made plans to get together as often as they could.

The kids at school noticed the change as well. When the four boys entered the building together, eyes bulged, and jaws fell open as they walked to their homerooms. Ryan turned to Jake. "I wonder what they are staring at?"

"I'm sure they are as confused as you were a few minutes ago," Jake replied.

At first no one had the courage to ask Jake about his face. Many of the smaller kids approached Ryan at recess and asked, "What happened to Jake's face?" The boys huddled closely, surrounding Ryan.

"Ask him yourself," Ryan replied.

"No way!" one of them said. "He'll pound us!"

Ryan calmly replied, "Ask him. I think you'll be surprised." Ryan smiled at the curious but terrified group of boys that surrounded him. "Fear of failure can be an emotion that will keep some people from doing what they want to do. Or that same fear of failure can be an emotion that pushes you forward and helps you to succeed. Which one will it be for you?" Ryan finished. "Go on. Ask him."

Jake, walking the perimeter of the playground, noticed one boy had finally mustered up enough courage to approach him. The youngster headed for Jake. Jake stopped when he saw the boy coming in his direction. He could tell he was nervous. Ryan and the others watched from a short distance.

"Hey, uh... Jake, what happened to your face? I mean, uh, are you okay?" The boy spoke so quickly that Jake didn't understand the words. Jake squinted his eyes and looked confused. The boy then pointed to his own face. "Your face. What happened to it? How did you get those scars?" The boy finally slowed his question and his breath.

Jake stared at the ground for the longest time, gently rubbing the enormous scars on his cheek. He looked up and nodded to Ryan. Ryan smiled back.

Jake walked to the closest bench and invited the boy to sit. Then he motioned to all the boys who were watching intently. Quickly, eagerly they shuffled over to the bench and sat down.

All eyes were fixed on Jake as he began the story.

"It was a blur. Riding down the road on a day of driving rain. The wipers could barely keep up with the amount of water on the windshield. Puddles on the road were like small ponds. I thought we needed a canoe, not a car. We plowed right through one of the puddles. The next thing I knew, the car spun wildly out of control," Jake explained. All the boys were on the edge of their seats hanging on every word, wanting to know what happened next. "The car hydroplaned on the surface of the water!" Jake paused, thinking of what to say next. One boy closed his eyes as his mouth widened. Another gasped and swallowed hard.

"The car stopped suddenly with a thunderous crash! I felt a warm sensation on my face. I tried to wipe the water from my forehead and cheek. Nothing helped. It wouldn't stop flowing. I couldn't see out of one eye. And the other was blurry. My legs were caught, trapped beneath the seat. My car door opened, and someone pulled me out," Jake spoke earnestly as the others hung on every word.

"I saw something cover my face and then things went black. When I woke up I was in the hospital, bandaged, with stitches in my face."

"Do you know who pulled you from the car and covered you up?" another boy asked.

"No. I didn't see his face. But later at the hospital a nurse told me that whoever it was saved my life," Jake nodded at Ryan.

"How?" asked the boy next to Jake.

"Just after he pulled me from the car, it caught on fire. Even the driving rain couldn't dampen the intense flames. The seat where I was sitting was destroyed before the firemen could put it out." Jake told the story with such detail, the boys took it all in, believing every word.

"I think I heard about that on the news," one boy said. "That guy's a hero," another boy whispered. Jake heard the whisper and commented, "He is a hero indeed, braver than anyone I have ever known. To this day, the identity of that person remains a mystery."

The bell rang, and the boys sprinted to the doorway. Jake shoved Ryan a little and asked, "How'd you like that story?" Ryan smiled. "Quite an imagination," he replied.

That summer was the best of Ryan's twelve years. He joined the local Little League, upon Jake's request, of course. Even though he wasn't on the same team as Jake, the two practiced together every day. Sam and Vince joined as well. The four boys met almost every single day at an empty lot next to the candy store and played ball. Jake taught Ryan how to pitch. Ryan taught Jake patience. When it rained, Ryan insisted they all meet at the library where his mother worked. They would gather around Jake's computer and watch highlights of their favorite baseball players.

The four were as close as brothers. There was no mention of the Seasons Away or the "dream." There was no need. What had happened was always in the back of their minds. The boys would never forget the experience that had brought them together.

CPSIA information can be obtained
at www.ICGtesting.com
Printed in the USA
BVHW071831040219
539420BV00003B/4/P